THE KING'S BANQUET

Derek Gorman

CONTENTS

PREFACE

B ased on Actual Events. What does that mean? It's a phrase often used by Hollywood, with differing interpretations. At one extreme it might mean that a King James VI existed in the 16th Century, and that's all. You'll be pleased to read that I've taken a stricter interpretation, and it has taken me a year of research to prepare this historical fiction based novel. In fact, this could probably never be made into a Hollywood film as they would edit and cut it too much; "remove the smoking", "why are they eating so much sugar!" or "do we really have to have him murder his mother in chapter one? That's a bit of a downer." but I care too much about accuracy and facts to let that happen - well, maybe an indie film is a happy compromise further down the line.

So what is true in this novel? Well, the characters that you will read about all existed, as did their back stories. Some of what you will read about will seem pure fiction but the characters have been chosen for their interesting lives so rest assured that those backstories really happened. Their character traits, where historically possible, have also been crafted to be as accurate as possible. Political events of the day are true. The events in this novel centre around one night at Knockhall Castle

- that night is documented as having happened - although we don't have details of the exact attendance and what events unfolded.

The payback from this novel is that while the events at the Castle are fictional - the ending is completely true. The lives that the characters end up living, the decisions & impacts that King James VI takes later on in his life, as well as the impacts on ordinary citizens are all real. I have crafted the events of the night in question in such a way to link it to the real outcomes that happened in history. And thus, this historical fiction novel *based on actual events* was born.

If you end up enjoying this novel, then leaving a review on Amazon is the best way to help me and show that you appreciated the amount of research and time this novel took to write. A follow up will also be in the pipeline based on a different historical time period. At the end of this novel if you would like to see photos and potraits of the people, places, and events that occurred then please visit my website www.derekgorman.com. Now sit back and step back in time to 1589...

I

Before the Banquet

CHAPTER ONE

JUNE 1589

One Month Before the Night in Question

It was a tense time in Scotland. Peace with England had been brokered three years earlier, but not all were in favour of closer ties with the 'old enemy'. Especially given the recent disaster of the English Armada. The more well-known Spanish Armada took place a year earlier and was an attempted invasion of England by the Spanish. They were soundly defeated by the English. Although, it was actually the Scottish that delivered victory given that the Spanish Armada ran into trouble on the rough Scottish seas and sank on the rocks. Boosted by this victory, Elizabeth I launched the English Armada to invade Portugal. King James cajoled Scottish businessmen to invest in this venture privately, all of whom were Lords, and most of whom were part of the Privy Council of King James.

It was therefore a difficult Privy Council meeting given that the English Armada were humiliated a few months earlier and there was massive discontent amongst the Lords, who were as a result significantly out of pocket.

King James was 23 years old and still forming his leadership style. His Privy Council was an important fortnightly gathering of those who effectively owned, and ruled, all of Scotland. It was no place for a young King to make enemies. King James wasn't blessed with a great physical presence; he was only 5 foot 4 and looked distinctly unremarkable, didn't look regal. and didn't speak like a Royal King. All he had was Royal blood, so how he handled these meetings were of grave importance.

This Council meeting took place at Holyroodhouse, one of several palaces that the King used as bases for his travelling Court. It was an exceptionally scorching summer in Edinburgh so it was no surprise when the King left the meeting room sweating. However, it wasn't just the heat, but it was also the tense atmosphere that caused it. He left the room accompanied by his closest confidant, Lord Sinclair, who somehow had refrained from perspiring.

"How do you manage to stay dry?" puzzled the King. "All future meetings that take place in this stifling heat will have to take place at Edinburgh Castle - the altitude and stone will make it a cooler setting."

The diligently loyal Lord Sinclair responded, "Of course, Sir. Truth be told, I felt the heat in there as well. I fear that it will not only be your neck on the line, but mine as well."

"It's a gruelling time," King James said. "Everyone is baying for my blood, but I want to celebrate next month - there are too many milestones for them to pass without an epic celebration. We need to be mindful though that it isn't seen to be too over the top. Events with Mother are still on people's minds too."

The peace treaty brokered at Berwick three years earlier was truly historic, not only would there be peace between England and Scotland but it also led to a path for King James VI of Scotland to become the first ever King of both Scotland and England. For James, this meant everything. He even turned a blind eye to the murder of his mother, Queen Mary of Scots, a year later. He viewed it as a necessary act by Elizabeth I to ensure she remained in power until her death, which opened the door for James to truly control the entire British Isles. There was also a financial benefit for King James, he would now receive an annual pension from England as part of the agreement.

The King hadn't yet celebrated his eventual rise to the English throne given that his Mother's death took place not too long ago. It just wouldn't have felt right. This year would also be extra special because King James was getting married, so this celebration would not only commemorate the deal signalling his path to becoming King of England, but also of his marriage to Anne of Denmark.

King James continued, "Given the financial losses that the Lords and Barons have taken because of this English Armada fiasco, we need the night to be discreet."

The King's sensitivity towards the mood of his Lords shouldn't have been a surprise. Kings were rarely dictators and had to hold together the fragile relationship between Lords and Barons along with the Crown.

James's family life had also been anything but stable. He became King of Scotland aged only 13 months old when his Mother, Queen Mary of Scots, was forced to abdicate. The circumstances around her abdication were complicated.

Mary was forced to marry Lord Bothwell, who took a divorce from his existing wife only 12 days earlier. Given that divorce wasn't recognised in the Catholic world, the marriage took place under Protestant rites. This didn't go down well with the Catholics who viewed Lord Bothwell's divorce unlawful and therefore the Protestant marriage to Queen Mary as being invalid.

Mary also upset the Protestants, as Lord Bothwell was the man who was the prime suspect in murdering King James's father and Mary's first husband. The murder was obvious given that he died through two explosions which took place below his sleeping quarters. Bizarrely, he was already thought to have died from strangulation before the explosions took place. All of this saw Queen Mary being branded an adulteress and a murderer. She was therefore forced to abdicate. Lord Bothwell was forced to flee Scotland. He ended up in Denmark where he was imprisoned, became insane and died a few years later.

All of this upheaval leaves a lasting mark on a child, so it was no surprise that the King knew that to remain in power for a long time required a potent mix of arrogance and political Machiavellian manoeuvring.

Stag parties were also nothing new. Celebrating a man's rite of passage to marriage was something that the ancient Spartans did in 5th century B.C. with banquets. Henry VI's also enjoyed the tradition through epic feasts with dancing and drinking. King James therefore expected an event suitable for his status and stature. A night to forget about the financial (and political) disaster of the English Armada. The pressure was therefore on Lord Sinclair to make this the event of the century.

Lord Sinclair felt the importance of the event so reassuringly said, "I will host the celebration personally and it will be an honour to have this take place at my recently built Castle, Knockhall. Rest assured that in a month's time - you will have an event worthy of the momentous occasions that we are celebrating."

A memorable night was therefore all but guaranteed to occur...

CHAPTER TWO

Lord Sinclair was an elder statesman, aged 62 years old. He was tall and handsome when he was a younger man. His frame now slightly crooked as he walked, adding a feeling of fragility. His face full of wrinkles told of a man who had already lived one life's worth of adventures. Married to his first wife, Janet for over 20 years - her death 20 years earlier was an event he thought he would never overcome. The four children that they had together reminded him of Janet every single day, and the knowledge that the lineage of the Sinclair clan was in safe hands was reassuring. This Lord was the 5th Lord Sinclair. His father passed away a while ago and had a colourful life - being arrested for treason, so often the case if you choose the wrong side, but luckily he was given the chance to see the errors of his ways and chose the right sides in future political struggles.

Lord Sinclair was an impeccable friend and loyal servant to the Scottish Crown. He signed a bond of loyalty to Queen Mary and King James's father before James was even born. He was part of King James's Council from day one of his reign when James was merely 13 months old. His loyalty to the King continued to be shown throughout the years.

He also supported him during the Raid of Ruthven. When the King was only 15 years old - he was kidnapped by an army of 1,000 rebels who supported the return of Queen Mary and wanted to limit pro-Catholic and French influence. King James was held captive for nearly a year moving from house to house. The plot was successful, partially funded by Queen Elizabeth I, who supported the rebels. Eventually, the King's supporters freed him displeased by the interference from England and he escaped regaining control. James showed a kind, or weak, side pardoning all those who plotted against him as long as they showed loyalty going forwards.

Lord Sinclair was also a key part of the negotiating team that sealed the treaty of Berwick paving the way for James to become joint King of England and Scotland. James looked at Lord Sinclair as a father figure in some ways - not knowing what a father or mother figure should really be or act.

Lord Sinclair's family life was happier too. He had just celebrated his one year wedding anniversary with Elizabeth Forbes, who was some 20 years younger, and had given birth to a little baby boy.

It would therefore be an epic celebration for King James and for the Sinclair family. This would be an enormous event, and even though he had seen and done this many times before, he was nervous. He was nervous because he felt Scotland, and King James, was changing. He wasn't sure exactly where this was headed but there was discontent brewing amongst the nobility in the land - and King James was now into his twenties and who knew how he would develop. Lord Sinclair feared he would try to rule with an iron fist and he had seen too often that strategy fail. But all these fears had to be parked for now to ensure that the banquet went ahead with no hitches.

However, there was already a major hitch. Wine supplies were very difficult to get hold of. The Royal Household had financial problems. King James liked to live like a King and whatever budget he would have, he would spend one Merk more (Merk was the Scottish currency before it's union with England).

James's response was always "I need to live like a King. That is the way King's get respect and nobody will become King of England by being financially prudent. They need to see me as an equal to Elizabeth's extravagance. They need to see me as deserving the throne."

In some ways, Lord Sinclair agreed with that strategy so he had to accept this paradox, which meant financial prudence went out of the window - but that didn't help to get wine supplies. The Royal Household frequently paid suppliers late, if at all. The suppliers therefore tried to avoid supplying the Household if they could. Messages were always lost, orders misplaced, and deliveries "delayed". After all, a supplier couldn't take the King to Court for non-payment. However, Lord Sinclair knew everyone and his elder statesman role meant he could call in a favour, which he did, he was granted 100 bottles of the finest wine for the event but he knew that, besides ensuring payment was made, he would have to repay the favour sometime.

One item that wasn't in doubt and didn't require any favours was the choice of venue. It would be the splendid Knockhall Castle. Finished only 4 years earlier, it was a masterpiece in design - relatively compact compared to the more lavish palaces of the era. What it lacked in size, it made up for in charm. Knockhall was close to Newburgh, the popular coastal village within Aberdeenshire.

Newburgh had picturesque beauty. Full of rolling greens and trees with only a sprinkling of houses. Sandy dunes reached into the sky almost as high as volcanoes, which shielded the beaches from the elements. It was the perfect country getaway, subject to the temperamental weather. Fishing was the chief industry with the River Ythan providing fresh Scottish Salmon for the Scottish nobility, whilst also providing a valuable trading commodity with England and France.

Newburgh was also heavily linked to the Sinclair family. The village was originally founded when one of the Lord's ancestors wanted to start a church in the area and so the Sinclair link was born.

It was therefore with an element of pride that Lord Sinclair looked forward to hosting the King at his Knockhall Castle. It was built as a gift for his first son, who would eventually inherit the lineage, but for now it remained his home when he wasn't travelling with the King across his collection of palaces. The history books would record King James VI visiting on the 9th of July 1589. That was now only a few weeks away and Lord Sinclair really was anxious.

King James had lofty standards. This happened when you lived across six palaces and had a Court travelling alongside you. It was a Royal version of a travelling circus. Countless servants, Lords, cooks, maids, administrators - all packing up and moving whenever the King felt like a change. His palaces included the impressive Holyroodhouse, Edinburgh Castle, and his personal favourite, Stirling Castle.

Knockhall was compact, but it had enough rooms to cope for the event. When you first made your way to Knockhall, you would see it in the distance as it had a dominating presence across the skyline. Visitors from miles away would see Knockhall half an hour before arriving. When you finally made your way to the front door, you would be greeted by a grand doorway, unusually built on a diagonal. Then you would walk down a red-carpeted, stone corridor, filled with grand paintings of famous Scots throughout history including the Sinclair clan. A spiralling staircase awaited at the end taking you up the tower and to the other levels. On the first level, you would be greeted by the banqueting hall. An impressive space in terms of design, if not size. A grand mosaic filled the ceiling - it was something you would see abroad and not on these isles. Lord Sinclair was very pleased with this - it was an acquisition he had made during one of his trips overseas. It had cost him £50 - a princely sum in those days given that it was enough to buy 9 horses or would have taken a skilled workman a year and a half to have earned that. The mosaic featured a heavenly scene with angels flying amongst birds with a powerful sunlight bursting through the clouds representing God's strength.

The second level had the four bedchambers - two masters, one for the Lord and one for the Lady, and two smaller ones, for guests. These were modern as they included latrines in each corner, and fireplaces to keep them warm in the bitter Scottish winters. The second level also had a dovecot, Lord Sinclair was fond of birds and in particular, messenger birds.

Lord Sinclair often remarked, "When a man reaches

my age, if he hasn't found a hobby then God will have other plans for him."

The birds were useful, although he only used it for pen pals in England, although he had started an attempt to get them to fly as far as France. The problem is getting them to return. Time would tell if he would succeed.

The top level then had an attic with another room that was small. It was his study, an oasis of calm away from the stresses of the Scottish Court and the demands of family life, although he was rarely here to use it. This would become a temporary bedroom for one guest.

The rest of the Castle had places that the King would definitely not see. The Ground floor was primarily working areas. There was a Kitchen, which had modern features such as a fireplace, sink and drain. The cellar was next door, which also had a sink and drains to protect the stores from flooding. A larder and pantry would complete the Ground floor ensuring enough space for storage of the vast quantities of wine and other delicacies that would make their way to the Castle.

"What a hive of activity it will be!" remarked Lord Sinclair to himself.

In the basement, there was the buttery and another cellar, and the servant quarters. Servants slept on mattresses stuffed with straw on the floor so it was little more than a cold, slightly damp room resembling a cave with no natural daylight. It would get quite stuffy on the night given the number of servants and staff required to service such an occasion.

Knockhall was therefore about to punch above its weight to host a grand event. It definitely wasn't Holyroodhouse - but Lord Sinclair was determined to ensure it held its own. Compared to the rest of Scotland in the 16th century, it was an oasis of extravagance. The country was primarily wet land and peat bogs that made travelling slow going. It therefore meant that the highlands were agricultural and why castles like Knockhall had a dominating position on the landscape, the simple fact was to stay out of the marshes you had to be on higher ground.

There were demands placed on Lord Sinclair for owning such vast amounts of land. He was obliged to plant trees and wasn't allowed to chop any down. This had little to do with environmental concerns and was more down to basic economics. Given the wet landscape, it meant that there wasn't an abundance of raw materials for building so a tree planting law was introduced. There was a three strike rule, the first time was a hefty fine if you were found guilty of cutting down a tree. A second time would result in a fine that even the richest Lord would have felt. A third time was a sign that you weren't listening so you would be sentenced to death. King James had already banned imports of Danish timber to Scotland to appease his future bride, Anne of Denmark, but this exacerbated the problem.

Scotland had a feudal land system. The King owned all the land but Lords had rental of parcels of land from the King. They then sublet it to freemen who were the merchants and workers that made the economy tick. The problem was that these freemen were mobile, travelling where there was money to be made so they never built permanent homes. They focused on temporary shelter and didn't look after the insignificant parts of Scottish land that were reality inhospitable.

It was therefore unsurprising that when visitors from England or France visited Scotland, they weren't impressed with the country.

"The villages look poor. They can't even build solid foundations," would remark one visitor.

"A few stones jumbled together is someone's home? This country has plenty of livestock and everyone appears well fed but it's clear that the only thing scarce here is money," said a visiting Doctor from abroad.

It is therefore in this context that whilst Lord Sinclair's home might not have been a grand palace that the King was used to. It was still very impressive when compared against the rest of Scotland. And for that he was proud of what he had achieved in his life, and of his family home.

II

The Banquet

CHAPTER THREE

THE DAY OF THE BANQUET
9th July 1589

L ord Sinclair awoke to a bright sunny day. An excellent omen that the day would be a successful one. It was only 8am, but there was already a lot of commotion. As he dressed and made his way downstairs, he could see that Lady Sinclair was already downstairs instructing the servants on where to place piles of fish and deliveries of flowers. Lady Sinclair was a family woman, she liked to take care of the children and was very loving to her husband. She was of average build and height with curly hair, which was unusual for the region. Her pale skin tone consistent with a life restricted to the Aberdeenshire winds.

She came from a good upbringing being the daughter of the 7th Lord Forbes. Her father was no stranger to royalty, holding the title of "Gentleman of the Bedchamber". A role that entailed being in proximity to the previous King whether that would include dressing him, waiting on him while he ate, guarding the bedchamber as well as providing general companionship.

She had spent all her life in Aberdeenshire, settling in

Newburgh with Lord Sinclair. She lived and breathed the area and wanted to play her part in ensuring King James felt that Aberdeenshire was the finest area in all of Scotland.

Knockhall Castle continued to be a hive of activity with comings & goings. The poets had arrived late last night, so Lord Sinclair didn't have a chance to greet them. They were in full voice outside the main door, so he went to welcome them to his Castle.

"Greetings and welcome to Knockhall," bellowed Lord Sinclair.

"Why, thank-you. You have a most marvellous home. May I say even delicious? Lady Sinclair is very lucky indeed" said the first Poet slightly unusually, both in tone and content. Lord Sinclair took this to be a sign of creativity and artistry, as he did the clothing. The poet wore tight trousers and a dishevelled shirt with three different necklaces around his neck.

"The name's Mark Alexander Boyd," said the first poet. *"Je suis ici pour divertir tout le monde. Le divertissement est ce que je fais. Je vis pour divertir!* I am just so full of life!"

Lord Sinclair knew of Mark Alexander Boyd. The King had a fondness for the arts and poetry in particular. Mark was 27 years old and dashingly handsome in a rugged kind of way. He was as thin as a match but he had a striking jawline that made the ladies swoon at his feet. He also had a way with words and had an exotic upbringing. He studied Civil Law in France - his intelligence and creativity becoming a very potent mix. He still lived in France and had even served in the French Army. He was as exotic as they came. He was sure to be a hit. The King, in particular, wanted to spread beyond these shores. Anything exotic always intrigued him, so it would be interesting to see what Mark had planned for the night.

After Lord Sinclair and Mark exchanged pleasantries, the second poet piped up, *"Je peux aussi parler français. Et moi aussi je peux faire des rimes et des poèmes de la beauté de la langue française!"*

Lord Sinclair didn't speak French, so he just looked there puzzled and startled. The two poets laughed amongst themselves before the second poet spoke, "How are you Lord Sinclair?"

"Very well, William. How is the Castalian band treating you?"

"It has changed my life in more ways than you'll ever know," beamed William.

The Castalian Band was a prestigious group of Poets and Makars (Royal Bards) who would travel and entertain the King's court. They were named Castalian after a spring of inspiration for poets in ancient Greece. The King inspired by the Italian Renaissance era imported as many ideas from abroad as possible. He didn't want to be a ruler of a country full of low lying wetlands, he wanted to rule a sophisticated, cosmopolitan, exotic, and cultured land - and he would do everything he could to turn Scotland into one.

Membership was fluid, but William had been a permanent fixture there over the last couple of years ever since writing *the Tarantula of Love* which made King James swoon at his talent.

William Fowler was 29 years old and, he too, was incredibly handsome. He wasn't very tall, standing at only 5 foot 6, but he made up for that with his strength. He was well built and looked like he could lift a horse with those big biceps of his. He had a weathered look on his face. A sort of charming rogue who had seen adventures beyond his years. His outfit was more conventional than what Mark wore - opting for the normal robes you would see on a gentleman of the day.

William knew French, as he too had studied Civil Law in France. This is where he first met Mark and their paths crossed over the years. He and King James were close. Rumours were rife about the nature of their relationship and Lord Sinclair knew all about that, but he dismissed it as cheap gossip. King James had beamed about William frequently mentioning how he had taught him the art of memory and how he in return had taught William all about poetry and emblems. Yes, that's correct, King James taught one of Scotland's most famous poets how to successfully write poetry. The King published a book five years earlier all about the rules of poetry, which became the standard for all aspiring poets in Scotland. This was besides his role as head of the Castalian Band.

Their friendship was strong and William's membership of the Band meant that he had readily available access to the King. The King bringing William into the fold made political sense, as William was one of Scotland's most famous poets of the time and he was vocally anti-Catholic criticising them frequently in his work. This played well with England and would be crucial to see James cement his place on the English throne.

"How was the trip?" asked Lord Sinclair.

"It was marvellous." replied William. "Not too many

people knew about it, but it was a splendid opportunity. As you know James and I have a very strong friendship, much like your relationship with James."

Lord Sinclair thought to himself that it wasn't quite the same relationship as he had with King James. He also didn't like the way William referred to the King as just James. Too informal, he thought. He was also disturbed that King James sent William Fowler to Denmark to arrange his marriage to Anne. It was too casual and just added fuel to the fire for the gossipers.

Lord Sinclair returned inside to the Castle and saw that it was noon. There was still no sight of the principal Actor of the evening. He was nervous about this as he didn't organise it. One message from William back to him was that Anne wanted to organise a minor surprise for the King and would arrange her own Actor to provide the evening's major entertainment. It was unprofessional and unusual for this man not to be here by now. In fact, he should have been here late last night like the poets. It's now midday with the banquet only hours away and he still wasn't here. Lord Sinclair went back to ask William about this.

"Do you know when the principal Actor will be here?"

"Ahh... he is a genuine artist. Honestly, you will have seen nothing like him. You may view me as a poet. Maybe even a talented one given my rise to the Castalian Band, but let me assure you, everyone will open their mouths in shock at this man's exceptional talents!"

"OK - but do you think he will make it here on time?"

"He will be here. Anne of Denmark is personally arranging it all."

Lord Sinclair shrugged and headed back inside. William's response wound him up even more. Anne was 'Anne of Denmark' but King James, who would soon be the first ever King of both Scotland and England, was just *James*. It was infuriating.

Anne was only 15 years old but had fallen madly in love. Dainty and fragile, as most inexperienced girls of that age, her presence led those around her to want to comfort her. Her early childhood was happy as she was raised by her grandparents in Gustrow. Gustrow was an idyllic place for a young girl. A small town in the German Republic with plenty of greenery for little Anne to run around and play in. The palace that she called home was built relatively recently in a German renaissance style. It dominated the skyline of the tiny settlement in which it was located. At five, Anne moved back to Denmark but continued her happy childhood uninterrupted until she blossomed into a woman attracting suitors from all over Europe.

Her mother, Sophie, brokered her marriage to King James. Sophie was around Anne's age herself when she married the 38 year old King Frederick II of Denmark. Sadly, last year was a tough one as the King passed away leaving Sophie to pick up the pieces after a 16 year marriage. A power struggle ensued with her brother to become ruler of Denmark. Ultimately, she lost out to her brother so Sophie had then dedicated herself into finding Anne the perfect husband.

King James was a big catch, especially after the Treaty of Berwick made news all over Europe with his impending rise to the English throne. Anne fell madly in love with him, embroidering shirts for him while awaiting their marriage many miles away in Denmark. She also had 300 tailors working on her wedding dress.

"Before I forget," mused Lord Sinclair. "How did the negotiations end with Denmark?"

"All resolved. We got what we wanted," confirmed William.

Royal marriages were difficult negotiations. The Dano-Norwegian Realm was a union comprising primarily Denmark and Norway who had finished a bloody and expensive war with Sweden several years earlier. The war was caused by Sweden splitting from the union decades earlier. The ramifications were still being felt, especially financially, with farmers fed up with the tax burden that they were being placed under.

It was therefore not an easy negotiation. King James was entitled to a dowry by marrying into the Danish Royal household, and Denmark believed they were entitled to regain the island of Orkney based on another dowry from 200 years ago. In the end, King James dropped his claim to a dowry from the Danish Royals, and Denmark dropped their claim to the island of Orkney. There were no longer any barriers to the marriage going ahead.

CHAPTER FOUR

THE GUESTS START ARRIVING
9th July 1589

I t was now mid-afternoon with the banquet due to start in two hours. The King would arrive last, so guests were expected to arrive shortly. The Castle was now an oasis of calm, and all the hustle and bustle of the morning had dissipated. Even the Lord & Lady had settled down and seemed quiet. Although that might have been partially because of the dram of whisky that he had just sampled, although there was no need to sample the whisky given, it was the finest that money could buy. However, he didn't want to appear as if he was drinking to calm his nerves so went through the rouse of sampling in case any of the servants were to catch a glimpse.

The Castle was now beautiful. Bouquets of flowers lined the corridor leading up to the banqueting hall. The floors had been cleaned spotless, and the musicians were already in place in the banqueting hall, waiting for it to begin. It was therefore time to start the pre-banquet arrival drinks and the obligatory small talk. Lord Sinclair didn't like this, as it usually involved some gossiping about the latest rumours about King James. Most of the time, these were scandalous and just absurd. The most recent one that Lord Sinclair had heard was that King James was learning French and was planning to give up the throne and move to France to become a painter! It was unbelievable stuff!

The first carriage to pull up was that of Andrew Melville of Garvock. It was a round top carriage which was standard of the day; it had one horse pulling it along with a carriage at the back with a wooden frame that created a round top. The enormous challenge on journeys such as this was the exposure to the elements. It wasn't a pleasant journey, but luckily Andrew didn't have to travel too far.

Andrew was a medium build man in his 40s with an unremarkable look and an unremarkable choice of outfit. He didn't come across as one of the power brokers or a *mover and shaker*. He was lucky to be here. Andrew was a loyal Master of Queen Mary's household, managing all of the different staff that would work around the clock to keep her Royal household ticking over. He really was trusted by Queen Mary, and accompanying her body to the cemetery was one of the most difficult, and saddest, moments of his life. He didn't have to worry financially because several years earlier Queen Mary bequeathed him a pension of 200 Merks per year, but it wasn't about the money. It was natural to feel her loss after spending over 20 years with her. And he did a lot more than just look after the household.

In 1571, he was sent to meet Queen Elizabeth's envoys to see whether peace could be brokered between England and Scotland. That failed, and the civil war continued for another 15 years until the Treaty of Berwick was signed - which tragically sealed Queen Mary's fate. He also fought alongside his brother in the Queen's forces. For example, he was in the final garrison defending Edinburgh Castle and was prepared to die for Scotland until the order was given to surrender.

When Queen Mary was in the latter stages of her life and exiled to England, he accompanied her and was in a position of immense trust, once being tasked with transporting £200 as a wedding gift. It would have taken a skilled workman six years to have earnt that sum.

In the weeks before her execution, Andrew was kept away as it would have led to them both being too emotional. He returned on the fateful day of her execution, where they shared some tears and final thoughts together. It was Queen Mary's wish that Andrew go back to Scotland and share her desire for a union between Scotland and England - she didn't want her death to put that in jeopardy. He did eventually return to Scotland, after being held captive for a short while to see whether he was actually a spy, and was snapped up by King James getting a further pension of 400 Merks per year. And so Andrew was now in the King's household. Even though King James had played a part in the downfall of his mother. Andrew believed that the King had little choice, and it was Mary's dying wish to see her Son rise to the throne of both Scotland and England. It was therefore a little unusual that someone in the King's employment would be invited to such a banquet but he had become one of the family and keeping him close reflected well on the King. The last thing King James wanted was for Andrew to become a spokesman for the rebels who supported Queen Mary. However, Andrew would never be viewed as upper class or an equal of the fellow banquet guests, and he knew it. It was therefore no surprise he opted to arrive first to the banquet as a sign of respect for the other guests.

Jane Melville was his wife and accompanied him. She too was in her 40s and had worked for Queen Mary as *Maid of her Chamber*. Another loyal and dedicated member of the Queen's household - she would keep the Queen company and guard her bedchamber. One perk of the role was being responsible for all of the Queen's jewels, and there were plenty to look after.

It is here where she first met Andrew, who was impressive - he had started in a similar position but worked his way up in importance to be an envoy for the Queen and Jane always had a crush on Andrew. He noticed her as well - red hair was rare and Jane was a fine beauty with her long red hair falling to the middle of her back. Andrew was smitten with her, but they did nothing about it. Life in the Royal household was too hectic.

It was only upon returning to Scotland they both decided to marry and start a family together. They were in a position of power, being entrusted to bring Queen Mary's jewels and artworks back to King James after her death. They had spent long enough working for others and would now look after themselves. Andrew was working for the King with Jane's support, but they prioritised time together above everything else. So when they arrived for the banquet - they were both appreciative that they had finally reached a happy point in their lives where they were comfortable and also knew what was important. They had also just celebrated their two year wedding anniversary, another occasion to celebrate at this banquet.

"Welcome to Knockhall," bellowed Lord Sinclair as he met the couple just outside the primary entrance.

"Thank-you Sir. It's very grand," replied Andrew nervously. It wasn't often that he was invited to an event like this almost as equals.

"Yes, it's lovely. You've done an impressive job with it," chimed Jane.

"You are all too kind. Look, just behind you. We have a fellow guest merely minutes behind," observed Lord Sinclair.

In the distance, not too far away now, was another coach, but this was very different to Andrew's. This was a 'four poster' carriage, which was a recent invention. It had a door and protection from most of the elements and was housed in a square box as opposed to their more basic round top cousin. King James used this, but it was relatively rare to see this outside of the Royal household. This would most likely be Thomas Randolph, or the Ambassador as he was known. He was coming all the way from London, so it wasn't a surprise that he was early given the time such a journey would take. As the coach approached closer, Lord Sinclair could see that it was indeed the Ambassador.

The Ambassador was an elder statesman. Now 66 years old, he really had lived a lifetime or two. Unfortunately, it showed. He was frail and hunched over his walking cane. He still had an impressive aura around him and would always wear the finest garments. He had that pride in appearance that those of advancing years always seem to have. The first half of his life had been relatively unremarkable. He was born in Kent, England and studied hard, eventually going to the University of Oxford, which then led to him becoming a notary. He did this until he was 30 years old before the Protestant prosecutions drove him away and he retired to France becoming a scholar. It was at 35 that his life began and became a lot more interesting.

Queen Elizabeth becoming ruler of England changed everything for the Ambassador. He quickly fell into favour and acted as a spy for the English in the German Republic. Little is known about what he did and he never spoke about it, so it remained a mystery. All that is known is that he returned to England after a few months and settled down in Kent. He remained valuable to Queen Elizabeth given the respect he had built up during his time in France with the Scottish protestants who had become a sizable expat community in Paris.

One of his missions was to smuggle in a Scottish nobleman into Scotland. He did so using the alias *Barnabie* and the code name *Pamphilus*, a likely nod to a biblical scholar who had lived many moons ago. Truth be told, that his genuine quality was his ability to influence the Scottish Protestants. They danced to his tune, and he brought them onside to follow Queen Elizabeth. The Ambassador therefore played a key role in the union's formation between Scotland and England. It is no exaggeration to say that without him the bloody civil war would still be raging. Hence the respect that he commanded. Lord Sinclair had goosebumps to think that the Ambassador would be here in mere minutes, what an honour it was given his fragility and age.

The Ambassador was central to some of the juiciest

gossip of recent history. While Queen Mary was still powerful and Queen Elizabeth's influence was only starting to grow, the Ambassador was tasked by Elizabeth to complete the marriage of Queen Mary to a suitable husband. Elizabeth was in love with a man called Robert Dudley, but with her health in doubt, she wanted him to succeed to the throne so proposed Dudley as the future husband of Mary and instructed the Ambassador to "get it done." Elizabeth wanted Mary to marry Dudley and for all of them to live together in the English Court. Mary wasn't sure about this as it sounded like a trap, but potentially being given lineage to succeed Elizabeth as Queen of England was something she would be interested in. Dudley was then made Earl of Leicester to make the marriage more attractive in Mary's eyes. The Ambassador was central to these negotiations, and eventually Mary agreed after several months of hesitation. However, Dudley refused. He wanted to marry Elizabeth and still believed that possible. That never happened, as Elizabeth couldn't marry an Englishman if she wanted a union between England and Scotland. Dudley died last year from stomach cancer. He married twice during his lifetime, but nobody who was anywhere near to the throne. How history would have been different if Dudley agreed to marry Queen Mary. Queen Mary might still have been alive and might even have become the first Queen of both Scotland and England. The Ambassador being the key pawnmaker. How Lord Sinclair would have loved to have heard the details of all these shenanigans - but of course, the Ambassador was discreet and never spoke of what he saw.

The Ambassador's life then turned another corner when he became *Postmaster General,* in charge of all the communications across the land and for the Royal household. This was a relatively calm year before his life would take another unlikely turn. This time he ended up in Russia on behalf of English merchants who wanted better trading privileges. He really had a gift of getting things done, and it was no surprise when he came back and the formation of the Muscovy Company was announced. It was one of the first major public stock companies in the world, and it had a monopoly on trade between England and Russia.

After his Russian adventure, he returned to Scotland and got married to the lovely Anne Walsingham. At this point he was nearly 50 years old, but he still hadn't slowed down. After getting married, he became *Chamberlain of the Exchequer* for life, always on hand to advise Queen Elizabeth - albeit primarily on financial matters, given his uncanny ability in finances. He still led on more missions for Elizabeth in Scotland and in France, but given his advancing years they were less juicy than previously.

The Ambassador wasn't immune to scandal himself. Rumours were rife that he secretly married a second wife in the last few years. Single for almost 50 years and then two concurrent wives within the last 15 years - it really was something you wouldn't expect from someone as distinguished as the Ambassador. It was therefore no surprise when he stepped out of the carriage alone, without his wife (or rumoured second wife). After being greeted by Lord Sinclair, he slowly made his way inside.

The last guests to arrive were Lord & Lady Maitland - they too had a 'four poster' horse drawn carriage that protected them from the elements. This really impressed Lord Sinclair. It was one thing for a King to have one, it was another for an Ambassador with international political connections to have one, but Lord Maitland's one was a clear statement of wealth.

Lord Maitland had turned 50 years old not too long ago and was on the slightly chubby side. He looked decadent with a pointy moustache complimenting his extended jawline. He was dressed impeccably, and you could tell that he was an important man, cultured too. He was another of those who had studied abroad in France before returning to begin his climb up the political ladder.

At the start, he didn't have to work too hard as he inherited his influence and power from his Father, including the role of *the Keeper of the Privy Seal of Scotland*, this was a powerful and important role. He would hold on to the official seal of King James and any document that would require the King's approval would require Lord Maitland to stamp it. Given that King James was only a baby at the time, it made Lord Maitland the de facto King. There were so many warring factions at the time, it was a fragile power, so he really didn't feel like a King.

Things quickly deteriorated, and his decision to back Queen Elizabeth in the civil war backfired. He was imprisoned for years and stripped of all of his titles and wealth. Quite a downfall from someone who was the de facto King.

He wouldn't have been a Maitland if he didn't have political cunning. As the civil war was winding down, he weaned his way back into favour with King James and regained all of his old positions, titles, and wealth. It wasn't just down to King James showing forgiveness to his enemies as part of the peace deal, but Lord Maitland had become powerful in England and King James was thinking about his future path to the English throne.

He therefore returned to play a powerful part in King James's court, much like he had when the King was just a young boy. Ever since his return to favour, he had been picking up titles all over the place becoming *Secretary of Scotland* five years earlier, followed by *Lord Chancellor of Scotland* three years ago and then the *Barony of Stobo*.

This created a lot of resentment and riled up some powerful enemies. Only a few months earlier, several Earls held a rebellion with plans to execute him and take control over the King. They marched to Holyroodhouse and won a powerful battle over the soldiers stationed there. However, their plot failed, and they were flabbergasted to find that the King and Lord Maitland weren't there. They were actually at Stirling Castle at the time, a benefit of the King's travelling court. When word reached the King about this plot - the rebels were soundly defeated. It wasn't the first plot to get rid of his influence - but they all had failed.

Lady Maitland was in her mid 30s but looked much younger and was stunningly beautiful. The stereotypical trophy wife with her long brown flowing hair; big brown eyes that melted many hearts. She had a face that showed little sign of life's struggles and had a svelte frame of a body. She had a reputation that meant most of the women weren't too friendly to her - many scared that she'll corrupt their husbands.

However, Lady Maitland came from a noble upbringing. Her father was the 4th Lord Fleming. Long before the scandal involving Queen Mary and her desire to marry

Dudley, she actually had a first husband. She married a King of France many years earlier when he was only 14 years old and she was only 16 years old, although he passed away only two years later. Lady Maitland's father was part of the delegation who attended the wedding in France. However, half of the eight strong delegation died on their way back after being poisoned. The French wanted to send a message that they didn't trust them.

This turned Lady Maitland's life upside down. She was only 5 years old and lost most of her inheritance to a greedy uncle. Life was therefore tough, and it is no surprise that she made the most of her noble background and her beauty. She was such a beauty that William Fowler had dedicated a poem to her *Triumphs of Petrarke*.

It was therefore no surprise that as Lord & Lady Maitland made their way to the banqueting hall that it should be William who they run into first.

"Bello come una rosa," bellowed William in Italian. *"Bello come un narciso. La bellezza arriva e la bellezza vede. Che bellezza avevano visto i miei occhi,"*

"William, you old charmer," responded Lady Maitland, whilst giggling.

Lord Maitland smiled and shook William's hand. William was an icon of Scotland and one of the most famous artists in the land, so his flirty compliment to his wife was viewed as a compliment. He also did that with all of the important people's wives but never overstepped the mark so wasn't viewed as a threat.

All was set. The guests had arrived. The flowers were in position. Music was being played. The kitchen was a hive of activity. It was now just time for the principal guest of the evening to turn up, King James, for his unofficial bachelor party / celebration.

CHAPTER FIVE

It was quite a scene in the banqueting hall as the pre-dinner drinks were being served. A bevy of servants patrolled the floor to ensure there was plenty of wine, whisky, or beer flowing for the guests. The hall really was ornately decorated. There were flowers across both long sides of the hall. Mosaics lined the hall, bringing colour and light to proceedings. The banquet table must have been 30 feet long. As was customary, benches lined both sides of the table. The only chair was placed at the end of the table, obviously for the King to use.

The guests and performers had split into two distinct groups. On one side of the hall, you had Lord & Lady Sinclair discussing political events with Lord & Lady Maitland. At the other end, you had the poets Mark and William standing alongside Andrew & Jane and the Ambassador. During the conversations, servants would top up quaiches (a small wooden shallow bowl with handles) with alcohol.

Mark said to the group, "I wonder which version of James will turn up."

"What do you mean?" responded the Ambassador, taking the bait.

"Well, who will be the Esme Stewart of the evening!"

"Esme Stewart? You mean the Duke of Lennox. What's that got to do with anything?"

"You've been out of the loop for too long, old man" replied William in a condescending tone. "Andrew, Jane - am I right?" The Melvilles nodded in agreement.

Esme Stewart, or the Duke of Lennox as he was now known, was famous amongst the King's inner circles. The King was a young man of only 13 years of age when he first made his way to Edinburgh Castle. Young and impressionable meant that he was easy prey for Esme. Esme was 37 years old at the time and married with five children. He had just arrived from France and was the most exotic thing that the King had ever seen; Fragile and tall like a bean pole, but he really intrigued the King. He was articulate, cultured, sensitive, spoke four languages and had life experience. The French just had a way of carrying themselves. They also believed themselves to be better than the English or Scottish, given their sophistication and culture. The King quickly brought Esme into his court and immediately gave him a senior role appointing him *Gentleman of the Bedchamber,* a role that involved Esme spending evenings and nights with the King. This would cover everything from keeping the King company to guarding over him while he slept.

Rumours about their relationship reached a new level when the King would be seen at banquets gently clasping Esme by the neck and kissing him passionately. The relationship grew and Esme quickly become an Earl and then the Duke of Lennox, a newly created title just for him. The Royal status benefited Esme socially and led to him being treated semi-seriously, as opposed to just a punchline in a scandalous bit of gossip.

His influence on the King kept growing, and it was when Esme entered the political sphere that it alarmed those close to the King. The Earl of Morton ended up almost executed because of a dispute with Esme. This was the turning point in the pair's relationship. The Raid of Ruthven that took place when the King was only 15 years old was partially down to limiting pro-catholic influence and bringing Queen Mary back to the throne but, truth be told, it was really a power struggle to limit French influence, Esme's influence. The King eventually agreed that Esme had to be exiled. He therefore returned to Paris. They continued their love affair via correspondence, but it wasn't to continue for too long as Esme passed away after only a year following a terminal illness. Esme's rise to the top and fall was only two years. Upon his death, his heart was transported to the King as per his wishes, although little is known about where the heart now lies.

"I have never heard something so absurd. A heart transported from the King's old male lover in a box all the way from France! You believe in fairytales," exclaimed the Ambassador.

"Say what you will but we all know it to be true," said a stern faced Mark.

At the other end of the room, the Lords, and Ladies were discussing the Ambassador.

"Did the Ambassador tout his ill thought out investment opportunity to you?" inquired Lord Maitland.

"Heavens, no," sputtered Lord Sinclair. "But I heard about it. It's a real shame what has happened to that fellow. He seems to have fallen from grace, and also what is he doing? Imagine coming to this event without his wife."

"Which one!" chuckled Lord Maitland, sending the rest of the group into fits of laughter.

The Ambassador had carried out many successful foreign trips on behalf of merchants with his Russian sojourn the pinnacle of his achievements. The Muscovy Company was doing well, and both Lords had a sizable investment in the company benefiting from generous dividends. However, that was more than a decade ago and the Ambassador was now an old man. He seemed to be missing the excitement of the past so was busy promoting an investment to set up an expedition to the New World. This was nothing new. It was nearly 100 years since Christopher Columbus's first voyage, and the entire region was still very volatile.

The Spanish had colonised parts of the New World and the last thing England needed was a bloody war with Spain in Europe, and in the New World. A private venture would therefore compete with all the difficulties of the time.

If you could get past the Spanish, then one problem would be the indigenous Indians. Over 8 million died because of European illnesses bought over by traders. They were therefore wary of anyone European. The *Lost Colony* was also a recent occurrence. The English had tried to establish two colonies in the New World. Both in Roanoke. The first attempt failed a few years back and the most recent attempt was a mystery - the entire population just vanished. Most likely killed in a bloody battle, hence it was now known as the *Lost Colony.* Therefore, any business investment opportunity to monetise the New

World was foolhardy. There was already a nasty feeling in the room post the English Armada fiasco, so there was little appetite to hear about the Ambassador's investment opportunities.

"What really concerns me is the state of the nation, I really fear for the King," mused Lord Sinclair.

"I agree," said Lord Maitland. "The finances are constantly stretched. Suppliers don't want to deal with the Royal Household. People are angry. And this impending marriage could be the end for the King, I fear. We are already financing one King with his travelling court and six palaces. The country cannot also finance a Queen with her own entourage and extravagances. The only hope is that the King takes the English throne soon and can subsidise his lifestyle through the English."

"They won't allow it. The English are too battle weary to allow extravagance from their monarchs. The days of Henry VIII are long gone."

At the other end of the room, Jane Melville was feeling envious of Lady Maitland.

"Look at her," remarked Jane. "She's stood there and thinks she can have any man she wants. I don't trust her. She's only with Lord Maitland for the money."

"The cat will take your tongue, Jane!" joked Mark to her.

"Sounds more like the cat, the panther, and the cockatoo will take her tongue!" contributed William.

The Ambassador clutched his quaiche tighter, probably wondering about whether his wife was with him for the right reasons. Perhaps he was merely wondering about the life that he was leading and wished for the woman he really loved.

His thoughts were interrupted as Lord Sinclair announced, "Men, smoking time".

All the men made their apologies and went upstairs to the drawing room that had been converted into a bedchamber for the night. Smoking was a popular pastime. Its popularity spread rapidly ever since Sir Francis Drake returned with tobacco from an expedition to the New World. A servant bought five pipes and a large handful of tobacco on a silver platter for the men to pick up. Each prepared their pipe before another servant lit it. The room was quickly dim full of smoke.

"This will help with my headache," remarked Lord Maitland.

"This will help with the cold I've been trying to shake off," contributed Lord Sinclair.

"This will get rid of that back pain," said Andrew, joining in.

"And this will help keep my energy up throughout the night, if you know what I mean!" William contributed crudely.

Tobacco was known as a cure for all ailments and a revolutionary medicine of the time. After a small period of silence, the Ambassador chipped in.

"Did you all know that tobacco comes from the New World? I've never seen an opportunity like this. Everyone was so excited about Russia, which was a monumental success - but this will be five times bigger. I've got..."

"Give it a rest, old man," interrupted Lord Maitland,

quite annoyed. "We've all been burnt by the English Armada. King James is taxing us to the hilt. His marriage will need paying for. And the New World is full of bandits, disease, enemies, and mysterious disappearances. Let's just enjoy this tobacco."

The Ambassador quietly accepted the interruption, but you could tell that he felt hurt. He also looked pensive, as if he knew that his glittering career full of golden contributions to Scotland was nearing the end.

"I don't understand why Elizabeth is persisting with this war on the Spanish," said Andrew to nobody in particular.

"Religion, my boy," said Lord Maitland. "Spain has their own problems as the Catholics are weakening. They see what is happening here, and they are afraid of Protestant influence reaching their shores. Elizabeth is equally frightened about losing control to the Catholics."

"Interesting, so when did the War begin?" asked Andrew.

"War has never been formally declared, it's just a dispute that started as a few battles and has now raged on escalating each time," answered Lord Maitland.

"You can pinpoint the start of the War, though," interjected Lord Maitland. "It started four years ago when some merchant ships were seized in Spanish harbours. It was a turning point as the English Privy Council approved retaliation off the coast of the New World, which was our first sustained activity in that part of the world."

"You see, the New World - all roads point there!" said the Ambassador.

Everybody groaned at that interjection but Andrew continued asking questions as he found it fascinating, "So what was the Spanish Armada all about?"

"Have you been on a farm for the last few years?" asked Willian, unhelpfully but everyone ignored him.

"Now - that is a very good question, boy," said Lord Maitland. "It all began when Mary was executed. Although everyone knew that Mary wanted to marry that Dudley chap - she eventually agreed to marry King Philip of Spain, who became King of England. Upon her death, Elizabeth claimed the throne from him and so it was full out war between the Catholics of King Philip and the Protestants of Queen Elizabeth. And we all know who won."

"You forgot to add the crux of the argument," interjected Lord Sinclair. "In the eyes of the Catholic church, Henry VIII never divorced Catherine, making Elizabeth an illegitimate ruler. The English Reformation began when Henry VIII wanted to break away from the Pope and Rome so he could get divorced. Under English religious beliefs, Elizabeth is a legitimate Queen."

A servant arrived and said quite nervously, "Apologies, everyone but we've just had word that the King will arrive here in a few minutes"

"Thank-you boy," said Lord Sinclair. "Now everyone please start to finish your pipes and then rinse out your mouth with wine or whisky. The King is not a fan of tobacco and I don't want him to make any of our lives difficult."

The conversation then turned to a lighter topic.

"Did you enjoy your round of Golf?" asked Lord Sinclair to Lord Maitland.

"I did, St Andrews is a stunning course," replied Lord Maitland.

"It is, nothing beats a day out on the course to get away from it all," said Lord Sinclair.

"I agree," chipped in Andrew.

Everyone was surprised. Golf was a game of gentlemen - how would Andrew have played golf?

"Which course did you play?" asked Lord Sinclair.

"Musselburgh Links was my favourite." said Andrew.

Lord Sinclair and Lord Maitland raised their eyebrows, astonished. Musselburgh Links was supposed to be the oldest golf course in the world. They wondered how he played there, but they didn't want to ask. Truth be told, it was Queen Mary who played there and Andrew was merely watching but he wanted to fit amongst the crowd so embellished his story a little.

With that, the men quickly finished their pipes and headed back downstairs for a dash of whisky, wine, or beer and then awaited the King's arrival.

CHAPTER SIX

The King Arrives

Six carriages arrived carrying the King, his close advisors, and servants. It was a procession with two of the carriages only used to carry the King's belongings such as robes, perfumes, and jewellery.

Everyone inside the Castle lined up in the corridor to greet and welcome the King. Lord Sinclair opened the front door and immediately stood next to the carriage. And he stood. And he waited. But the King was not leaving the carriage. Whispers began inside as to what might be the reason for the delay. Eventually, the door to the carriage swung open, and the King appeared.

The band of musicians had been positioned and immediately began playing some welcome music to make the King feel at home. There was no such thing as an official song of Scotland, so the band played a medley intended to inspire and energise the King.

King James was of average height but had bent legs that meant it looked awkward as he stepped forward. He was not a handsome man with a pointy chin and a goatee beard. His eyes looked dead inside with no sparkle. Slightly overweight as well did little to add to his charm.

"Welcome to Knockhall, your Majesty," said Lord Sinclair, bowing.

"Thank-you, apologies I'm a little late. I fancied a bit of Golf in the morning. Only managed nine holes, but now I'm ready to celebrate. Introduce me to everyone and then give me a tour of the place."

And with that, Lord Sinclair took the King down the line. First up was Lady Sinclair, who did the most elegant of curtsies.

"Lady Sinclair," began the King. "I'm glad you made an honest man out of this one and all the best on the one year wedding anniversary." The King's tones were warm, and he cradled Lady Sinclair's arm as he gave her the congratulations.

"Thank-you, your Majesty. Please do make yourself at home here and thank-you for gracing us with your presence," said Lady Sinclair with the King responding with a smile before moving firmly onto the next in line who was Lord Maitland.

"Maitland," said the King sternly. "Good to have you here. Let's talk about some business later."

"Of course, your Majesty. Next stop the World?"

The King guffawed at this comment and then moved on to Lady Maitland. She stood there radiant with a gentle smile and then curtsied seductively, if that were possible.

"Why Lady Maitland, you look more radiant than ever," observed the King.

"Oh your Majesty. You are too kind. I've been learning some poetry if the King would let his ears hear it later, but I'm too shy to have it heard in public so we must go somewhere private."

The King wasn't sure what to make of it. Was this an innuendo? But would Lady Maitland have done that in front of her husband? He must have been imagining it and assumed that were the case so he responded, "I'll squeeze you in but apologies in advance if my disposition perhaps cannot keep its promise later on in the evening."

The King shyly moved on to the next in line feeling very self conscious about his crooked walk and spotty face following the encounter with Lady Maitland. Next up was Andrew Melville. He curtsied.

"Thank-you," said the King. And with that, he was gone. Onto the next in line. Another painful reminder for Andrew that he wasn't the same as the other guests. Jane Melville received similar treatment with the King quickly passing her by after a momentary exchange of pleasantries. She seemed relieved at not having to make small talk.

He then made his way to the Ambassador who was hunched over and before he could curtsey, the King interrupted and said "Please don't, there is no need."

"Thank-you your Majesty, but I'd rather I did." And with that, the Ambassador did a half curtsey before making a slight creaking sound on his way back up.

He then continued, "I understand that you will have some private audiences tonight."

The King wasn't sure why the Ambassador said that.

He was here to celebrate, not to have a bunch of meetings. He figured that the Ambassador heard Lady Maitland's proposal. The Ambassador then continued, "It is of the utmost importance if your Majesty could spare me five minutes later to hear about a proposal of the greatest significance for Scotland."

"We'll see," replied the King before swiftly moving on.

Finally, it was the turn of the poets to greet the King. William was first, who did the obligatory curtsey.

"I see you've made it back from Denmark in one piece," enquired the King.

"Yes, what a strange place the Danish Kingdom is. Very different to Scotland. I must tell you all about it,"

"Yes, you must. Later, later."

And finally it was onto Mark. The ruggedly handsome poet who had an exotic upbringing stood there like a farmhand waiting to carry his crops. The King laid eyes on Mark and said nothing at first. His eyes started at his face, noticing his blue eyes and chiselled chin, and then made his way down to his torso and then all the way down to his feet. He then looked back into Mark's eyes.

"So you are this other poet I've heard much about?" asked the King.

"I wouldn't know what you've heard your Majesty. But rest assured, you will have heard about me by the end of the night."

The King wasn't sure what was going on. Why did everyone want private meetings with him? And was he really propositioned multiple times walking the line? Perhaps it was tiredness from the journey he had just taken. And with that, he beckoned to Lord Sinclair to give him the grand tour.

Lord Sinclair was a little self conscious as it was a rather small castle compared to the King's palaces. He led the King up the staircase to the banqueting hall, which was beautifully decorated. The musicians who weren't standing immediately did so and curtseyed from a distance. The King acknowledged them.

"This is the banqueting hall," began Lord Sinclair, much like a tour guide. "The room is obviously only one element of the evening. The people, the entertainment, and the food will make or break the evening,".

They then went upstairs to see the King's quarters for the night.

"You have my chamber for the night so please use this as if it were your own and let me know if there is anything else that is needed to make your stay more comfortable."

The King stroked his chin as he looked around the room. It was ample enough, so he waved his hand as a sign that this would suffice. Lord Sinclair looked pleased that the tour had gone well. This wasn't the most extensive of tours, but in reality a host could only show the King the best areas of the castle. Showing the kitchens or pantry was definitely not the done thing.

Before they returned downstairs, Lord Sinclair had one last surprise for the King. He pulled out a bottle of whisky from the Guild of Surgeon Barbers, Dundee. The finest producers of whisky in all of Scotland. It was their rarest bottle. The King's eyes lit up at seeing the bottle.

Whisky had quickly been welcomed into Scottish way of life after being discovered one hundred years earlier. What really give it a boost was the shutting down of monasteries during the Scottish Reformation which meant that monks had to figure out a way to make a living. Their solution was whisky production. The Guild of Surgeon Barbers was thought to produce the best because the only anaesthetic that a surgeon could give their patient would be a whisky.

"You have done well here, Sinclair," proclaimed the King. "A bottle such as this. Open it at once and let's have a taste."

Lord Sinclair did as instructed and poured two measures into quaiches for himself and the King. They both sat down and this offer of the finest Whisky had bought a private audience with the King, whether or not wanted. The King sipped his drink.

"So tell me, Sinclair," began the King. "As a father, do you feel that burden of responsibility? That you must do what is right even if your family cannot see the rationale for why."

"Yes I do," replied a considerate Lord Sinclair. "The role of Father and head of the household gives me the energy to do what I do. Whilst I appreciate our journey together, the reality is that providing my family the status that we have is the primary motivation."

The King didn't really appreciate this, thinking it was the answer of a simple mind. "I think you miss the point. Being a father is not about providing the best for the family. It is a duty to provide what the family needs. For example, Lord Newham or was it Lord Newsham, something or other, his son had the trappings of wealth and died at 17 due to foolish adventures. What he needed was an element of poverty. The role of Father is the same as my role as King. I don't have 2 or 4 children, I have over a million children. That is a burden. What you have are petty problems and a man's selfish desires to look after his own. I have a burden on over a million people. These are just laws of nature."

Lord Sinclair was a little surprised at the deep philosophical nature of the conversation given it was an evening of celebration, but he topped up both quaiches with the Whisky and then responded.

"I guess you are right. I cannot comprehend the level of responsibility that you have. It is something that someone like me could never understand."

That response was a smart political move by Lord Sinclair, as he knew that the King would lap it up.

"You are right," confirmed the King. "The other interesting aspect is the bond of love that I have with Scotland and that Scotland has with me. When I enter a town, people aren't on the streets because of fear or respect, whilst they do have those for my position, the real driver is the love they have for me. I am not a man but I am in this position thanks to God and no earthly being can judge me. The love that the people have is the same love that your children have for you, Sinclair. Sometimes they'll be cross with you, sometimes they will be happy with you. Ultimately, they love you. The people love me."

"I fully agree," said Lord Sinclair. He didn't really understand the grandiose statements coming, and he was sure that whilst some people loved the King, the majority simply accepted it as a way of life.

"The thing that makes me angry," began the King raising his voice, "are the people who opine on how I spend my money or the decisions I make in court. They do not understand their role. A son doesn't strike his Father. A son doesn't rise up against his father. Look at the animal kingdom, you see the paternal nature of all animals. There is only one animal that strikes against his own Father and that is the viper. The lowest of all animals. A viper. A reptile that signifies the biggest betrayal on earth. Lord Sinclair, are you a viper?"

Lord Sinclair was taken aback by this accusation. "Me, a viper? Sir, I have always been at your loyal command. Do you not remember how I signed a bond to you when you were merely 13 years old? Do you not remember how I supported you during the Raid of Ruthven? What about when I was part of the team to get the Treaty of Berwick signed only three years earlier to create your path to become King of Scotland and England? I have shown nothing but loyalty to you, your Majesty."

The King stood up and walked over to where Lord Sinclair was sitting. He had a stern look on his face and looked straight into the whites of Lord Sinclair's eyes. There was a momentary silence that seemed like an hour. The King then burst out laughing.

"You really are too easy to wind up," said the King. "I know all about your loyalty and I value it. Now pour me another."

And with that, Lord Sinclair had a slight grin on his face. A bead of sweat dripped off his forehead, which he wiped clear before pouring themselves an extra whisky.

The King then continued, "The fact that some people don't understand their love for me is down to the vipers on this planet but what really worries me is necromancy."

"What is necromancy?" interrupted Lord Sinclair.

"Necromancy is the prediction of the future by communicating with the dead," replied the King, surprised that Lord Sinclair didn't know. "Nostradamus is the worst. He pretended that his predictions were all because of astrology, but what a load of crock. The only way he can predict the future accurately is by communicating with the dead. They are on the other side and have access to things we can only dream of. I fear the other side. Homer unlocked this passage when Odysseus travelled to the underworld and now we have demons roaming alongside us with these witches, communicating with them and causing ghastly things to happen."

"I too fear them. The power of these witches needs to be curtailed. Why England repelled the Witchcraft Act for a few years before reinstating it is beyond me," said a puzzled Lord Sinclair.

The weather suddenly turned, and storms appeared on the horizon.

"Witches, even thinking and talking about them can conjure up some dangerous events," said the King. "Look at that storm. Some witch somewhere has brought that on the people of this area. That they can fly invisibly too means they are a threat to the land. I also don't like the celebrations with the chanting and dancing. They induce sexual deviancy in people. Who knows what goes in those potions?"

Suddenly a lightning bolt shot through in the distance, crashing through with a sound of thunder.

"Enough talking about these witches, let's get back to the party. I fear we are making things worse," said the King.

They then both headed downstairs back to the rest of the guests who had now re-convened in the banqueting hall.

Upon entering the hall, the King was still shaken by the discussion on witchcraft and the weather outside wasn't helping. He therefore had a bit of fun and beckoned the gentlemen to him, saying it was time for Noddy. He then headed back upstairs to his quarters with the Lords and the Ambassador following behind him. There was no place for Andrew, a reminder that whilst he might have been invited to this event, he wasn't one of them. The poets, whilst highly enjoyed by the King, were not aristocracy and were rarely treated as such.

Noddy was a popular card game at the time, where the aim of the game was to score 31 points and therefore get the noddy. A noddy was a fool or simpleton. The game was played in pairs.

"Come, you'll play with me," instructed the King to Lord Sinclair. "We'll take on Maitland and the Ambassador. Good luck chaps."

"Servant. Come," bellowed the King. Immediately a servant ran into the room with a cribbage board. A way of keeping score of the game.

"Right, let's begin. Usual stakes," said the softly spoken

King. Usually this meant £100 to the winning team and if the King lost, then he would fail to pay up, promising to send a servant with the cash in a day or two but then conveniently forgetting to ensure this happened. The King was famous for wagering on card games or on Golf but rarely paid out any losses.

The first part of the game was to see who would go first, so they would each cut the deck to see who chose the lowest card. First up was the Ambassador. He picked a King. Everyone chuckled. Then it was Lord Maitland's turn. He drew an eight. Lord Sinclair drew a nine. It was then the King's turn who picked a four and would therefore start the game.

Lord Sinclair dealt hands to everyone. Each player ended up with three cards each. There was one card in the centre which was a seven of hearts. The aim of the game was to get as close to 31 without going over. There was much commotion as players swapped cards and then the scoring begun. The King had 30. Lord Maitland had 27. Lord Sinclair 29 and the Ambassador refused to show his cards.

"First," began the Ambassador. "I must inform you all that whilst you may think of me as someone who has already seen their best days. My luck is just ahead of." He then guffawed as he threw down his cards. He had 31.

Everyone sighed and gesticulated wildly, as only the finest gentlemen could do after a few drinks of beer that were served during the round.

"Your majesty, I ask not of the £100 prize money but merely a two minute audience with yourself," enquired the Ambassador.

"Hey! What about my share of the £100?" asked Lord Maitland.

The rest of the gentlemen sniggered. Even one of the servants in proximity found it difficult to control himself.

"Nonsense, you will have the £100 but I will grant you a two minute audience regardless," said the King.

Whilst this was a generous gesture. Everyone knew that the money would not be forthcoming. The rest of the group therefore headed back down to the banquet, leaving the King and the Ambassador. The servants had left as well.

"Your Majesty, many think of me as an old fool, but the New World is the future. Mark my words, in times to come it will be an empire and frontier that will pave unlimited riches for he who is brave enough to conquer it."

This peaked the King's interest.

"Whilst the recent expeditions by the English have been unsuccessful," continued the Ambassador. "There is untapped potential. Previous issues have been the strategy taken. Guns or butter has been the problem. Previous expeditions have either been too focused on either the military side or the trading side. The solution requires balance. That way the indigenous people will respect and fear your armies but will welcome them for all that they can bring."

"Thank-you for bringing this to me, Ambassador. I know you have been mocked for your investment opportunity, but I think the Kingdom of England and Scotland will be the world's superpower. This Kingdom has been descended from God and I, like Banquo's descendants, will sit upon its throne. The world will then be ours." And with that the King went off back to the banqueting hall, leaving the Ambassador scratching his head. Banquo was part of *Holinshed's Chronicles,* a comprehensive description of English and Scotland's history published a few years earlier. In history, Banquo was a supporter of Macbeth helping him become King at the expense of King Duncan. The Ambassador wasn't sure why this was relevant. He figured that it was King James's belief that as a descendent of Banquo, the throne was rightfully his. And with that thought he eventually rejoined the main party downstairs.

It was now time for the part of the evening that the King particularly enjoyed. It was customary for an auction to be held before enormous events such as marriages, entries to positions of state, or baptisms. However, this wasn't a normal auction where Lords battled over paintings of landscapes or memorable war battles. It was a wedding auction. This is where the guests would battle over who would have the honour to provide, or pay for, certain items that would be used on the occasion.

King James was famous for being extravagant and spending all of his annual budget plus borrowing on top so occasions such as this that allowed him to gain further resources was a highlight for him.

Lord Sinclair gathered all the guests to the front of the banquet hall, where they stood with Lord Sinclair on a makeshift platform overlooking everyone. In his hand was a hammer which he banged against the edge of the table. He would be the auctioneer for the evening, a wise move as it meant that he couldn't take part in the auction himself. Although, there was an expectation that Lady Sinclair would bid on his behalf. This could have gone either way - she could be too feeble and therefore lose out in the bidding saving themselves a fortune or the complete opposite by not wanting to offend the King she may overbid and they will be significantly out of pocket.

"Lords, Ladies, and Gentleman," bellowed Lord Sinclair. "In honour of the King's impending marriage to Anne of Denmark, we will now hold an auction to allow people the privilege to either provide or pay for items that are required for the wedding. The first item is transportation. An important part of any wedding is the manner in which the bride and groom will reach the church. And a King and future Queen must travel in the manner they are accustomed to. Who will cover the cost of transporting Anne of Denmark and the King on the day of the wedding?"

"I will offer 2 horses," shouted the Ambassador, getting the bidding going.

"Do you expect the King and Queen to ride themselves to the Church?" Replied auctioneer Lord Sinclair mocking the bid. The Ambassador realising the error of his ways blushed with embarrassment,

"I will offer 2 carriages and 4 horses," offered Lord Maitland. A much better offer and more than sufficient for the travel.

"I will offer 2 carriages and 6 horses," responded Lady Sinclair. This was more generous, although carriages didn't need so many horses - it was a status symbol to have excess horses on one's carriage.

"I will offer 2 carriages, 6 horses, and 2 footmen," countered Lord Maitland. This would have been the clincher, thought Lord Sinclair.

"Right," said Lord Sinclair. "Do we have any more bids? Going once. Going twice. Sold. Well done to Lord Maitland, who has the honour of providing the transportation!

Now we move onto the next category, which is jewellery. As any female knows, a bride on her wedding day has dreamed of the moment she gets to drape herself in jewels from an early age. Just imagine the dreams that a member of the Danish Royal Household would have had as a young girl."

"I will offer to provide both rings," said the Ambassador, again being careful to be seen to be bidding but realising that he couldn't really afford to bid too much.

"You may have misheard me, Ambassador," said Lord Sinclair. "The King is marrying into the Danish Royal Household. Not a wench who served in the Nags Head pub on weekends."

Everyone sniggered at the lowball bid by the Ambassador and Lord Sinclair's merciless teasing of him.

Someone at the back chipped in and was heard sniggering saying "I don't think bronze rings are eligible."

"I will offer to cover both gold rings and a diamond for the bride," said Lady Sinclair. Lord Sinclair was pleased with this. It was an excellent offer but was likely to be outbid so saving them a hefty bill.

"I will offer to cover both gold rings, a diamond for the bride and jewellery for all the maid of honours," offered

William Fowler. The hall gasped at this offer. It was an enormous surprise that a poet could offer so much but poets were lauded as the superstars of the day so this would naturally have come from his admirers, maybe some of it from the King himself.

"Well. What an offer! Ambassador, are you paying attention? That is how it is done. I doubt we'll see any more bids? Going once, going twice. Sold!" said Lord Sinclair.

"Now we move onto the last category, the one we all love, which is Whisky and Wine. As we all know, you can't have a wedding celebration without some lubricant to make the evening go quicker. And on a momentous occasion, it won't be some swill bought from the Nags Head Pub that will be served. We need the quality stuff."

"One case of wine and one case of whisky," said the Ambassador, again being careful to be seen to be bidding but realising that he couldn't really afford to bid too much.

"Ambassador, you've made the auction," began Lord Sinclair. "I appreciate your bidding and thank-you for accepting the polite ribbing in the right manner."

The Ambassador didn't appreciate being patronised in this way, but he just bit his tongue and grinned politely.

"I will offer three cases of wine and three cases of whisky," said Andrew Melville, getting involved for the first time. Not a poor offer for someone who was an employee in the Royal Household.

Then it was the moment for Lord Maitland to get involved. He felt that William's offer in the last round had made him a star, which he didn't appreciate so he would not hold back.

"I will offer ten cases of wine, ten cases of whisky including one case of the Guild of Surgeon Barbers, Dundee, and five hundred thousand pints of beer - for the wedding and all of Scotland." said Lord Maitland to a stunned audience.

The King immediately came over to Lord Maitland, shook his hand and patted him on the back. It really was a very generous gesture, and one that cemented his status as one of the richest men in Scotland and one of the most influential men in the King's court.

"Well, unless the Ambassador has a counter offer, then I think we may be done. Ambassador?" asked Lord Sinclair.

The Ambassador shook his head, slightly annoyed that he was still the focus of people's amusement.

"That concludes the auction everybody. Please take your seats for dinner, which will begin shortly," said Lord Sinclair invitingly.

Everyone took their places on the benches, except for the King, who sat in his throne-esque chair. The music was playing, creating a warm atmosphere, and the audience were conversing amongst themselves. There was a hive of activity behind them with servants rushing all over the place. The weather outside had also improved with storms now just a distant memory. Stomachs could be heard rumbling, so the food arriving shortly would be perfectly timed.

CHAPTER SEVEN

THE MEAL

The servants were scrambling all over the place running from the inner courtyard up the stairs to the banqueting hall delivering knives and spoons. Each guest bought their own cutlery for an event such as this. It would have been an incredible faux pas to have forgotten or expect the host to provide one. Everyone's attention was drawn to the poet Mark. In front of him was a fork.

"What on earth is that?" asked Andrew who was sitting opposite him.

"Why, it is a fork. It's what sophisticated people in France use," replied Mark in a condescending tone.

There was a lot of aspiration in Scottish society and items from France were seen as sophisticated and exotic. Eating with a fork would be an exotic act that just made little sense to most people. The King from his seat at the end of the table cast a glance at this fork sitting on the table but said nothing. You could tell that he had made a mental note, given his love for all things French and exotic.

The love of France was really a nod to the power that the country had. Paris was the most populated city in all of Europe with their population reaching a mind-boggling 350,000. The Louvre was the King's official residence, and the City was beaming with renaissance style architecture. It was something that King James could only have dreamed about. The renaissance influence wasn't just limited to architecture, but it was also a cultural movement. The way people thought and were educated. The way international diplomacy was carried out. The way man thought about god, science, and art were all merged into one. It was an actual birth of a fresh way of thinking, a superior way. Paris really was a masterpiece and the heart of France. Only a year earlier, lanterns were being lit on every street corner at night to ensure visibility for all. That didn't even happen in Knockhall Castle - let alone in a city for 350,000 people!

It's true that France had its problems with the struggles between Catholics and Protestants but that was nothing unusual. Almost every country in Europe had those struggles, and it was expected that a country as special as France would be fought over. It was therefore this love of all things French that meant that Mark's fork was a hit, even if people didn't want to admit it.

The guests were all seated on benches either side of the King who was at the head of the table. It was now time for the Poets to make a welcoming speech. Mark and William stood up and burst into poetic speech.

"King, Father, Lord, God, Almighty One.

Thank the stars that bring us here.

A mighty sky, a bright dawn, heroic silence.

Breaks the waves, motioning down.

King, Father, Lord, God, Almighty One.

Let the Banquet commend everyone."

And with that - they bowed and awaited for rapturous applause for their latest poetic masterpiece. The guests duly obliged.

During the applause Lady Sinclair asked Lord Sinclair, "did that make any sense to you?"

"No, it's that typical pretentious artsy nonsense that sounds sophisticated because it's said with a Scottish-French accent," confirmed Lord Sinclair.

They both stifled a slight giggle before Mark sat down. William then announced, "I also have a special poem for the King but it is very exclusive, a gift from heaven, so only the King's ears may hear it. Your Majesty, if I may, please join me upstairs."

William then bowed awaiting the King's response. The King motioned his hand to signify his agreement, and he then followed William out of the room. William said nothing to the King but kept walking a few steps ahead of him. They went upstairs and ended up in the King's bed-chamber for the night.

William motioned for the King to join him on his bed and to get comfortable. William took off his jacket and stood a few feet in front of the King.

"Do you remember what I used to teach you?" asked William.

"How hilarious. Yes, you helped to improve my memory with your exercises," confirmed the King.

"Well, close your eyes and tell me... what colour are my eyes?"

"Brown," answered the King.

"And what are the size of my muscles?" asked William.

"Big," answered the King, slightly flustered.

William then took the King's hands and got him to feel his muscles. They were tense and showed the strength of a man who was artistic and yet could have been working on ships or doing manual labour. And with that, William suddenly changed direction and asked, "teach me some poetry".

During their sessions over the last few years, it was poetry that the King had fostered within William.

"Ok, any good poetry comes from the heart. So William what do you want?" asked the King.

"Ok... well in that case, how about this?

The dreams I have I see at night.

At night, the thoughts are all still and clear.

Jewels on my head and land beneath my feet."

"Not bad," said the King encouragingly.

And with that, William fell down into the King's arms and they both fell onto the bed lying down. They both giggled.

"You know William," said the King. "I really am fond of you. I want you to have that land beneath your feet one day. Maybe even a title too."

Meanwhile, downstairs back in the banqueting hall. Andrew and Jane were having a serious conversation away from the table.

"You should have told him," said Andrew.

"I can't, Andrew. You know what the King thinks about witches," said a worried Jane.

Jane then continued, "we would have lost our jobs and been sent away."

Only a few weeks earlier, while the Melville's were at home, there was a knock at the door. It was an elderly lady dressed all in black. She asked them whether they had any merks to hand out. Andrew always liked to help the less fortunate and handed her a few merks. She smiled and instead of thanking him, menacingly said, "Andrew, you may think you can buy forgiveness for your sins but betrayal speaks wise words and your family will be struck down. I place this curse on your wife. Your wife. Your wife." And with that, she gave off the most evil laugh and headed away from the property. Jane was in earshot and heard this before completely freaking out. To make matters worse, the sky had suddenly turned dark, and it rained.

Andrew tried to reassure Jane, "I think you are over-reacting, you know that he really appreciates our long service to his mother and our loyalty to him. Look he even invited us to this event."

"This event where we aren't treated as equals? And he will appreciate our service to his mother. Andrew, he signed her death warrant." replied Jane sternly.

"Excellent point."

Witches were an enormous problem in Scotland. Andrew knew all about them through King James. The King had a huge fear of witches so Andrew became familiar with the signs.

There were many of them in the poor infested villages and many ways to identify one, such as women owning a cat. Cats were rare and only appealed to witches. That's why dogs are a man's best friend, and why Kings only kept dogs. Anyone with a mole or birthmark on their face was being branded by the devil as having mystical powers. The biggest test was when witches were thrown into the river to drown - if they floated on water then they had mystical powers. If they drowned, then it turned out that they weren't witches after all.

The woman who had visited them had a mole on her face, something that Andrew noticed but it didn't strike an immediate connection as to what it meant. He regretted not shutting the door to her when he noticed but his mind wasn't quick enough, and now poor Jane was in a state of mental anguish.

At this point, the King, and William had returned from the bedchamber.

"An amazing poem, thank-you William," proclaimed the King.

They both sat down, as did the Melville's.

Next was the turn of the musicians to entertain the guests. They moved from being in the background - they stood at the other end of the table to the King with the silence palpable. After a few moments, they began with a melodic hymn that wouldn't have been out of place on a summer's day such as this - although it was now evening. After a few minutes, they received polite applause appropriate for such a refined performance. They then made their way back to the shadows where they would continue being the background music for the event.

Now was the moment that the servants were due to bring the food out on platters but nothing was happening. Everyone was busily talking amongst themselves but slowly one-by-one they were getting agitated. Lord Maitland started to sweat with beads running down his forehead. The King shot him a look that spoke a thousand words. Lord Maitland immediately hurried downstairs to the Kitchen to find out what was going on. There were a lot of servants and they were standing leaning against walls; some were smoking tobacco. One thing that definitely was not happening was any kind of activity underway to deliver food. Lord Maitland asked his Head of the Household, "What is going on? Why has everyone stopped?"

The Head of the Household looked sheepish saying, "Lord Maitland, you have been good to me and I will always support you. The problem is the extra servants that we have brought in here to help with tonight's banquet. They are part of the Royal Household and they have had no kind of pay increase for years and their living conditions have deteriorated. They have all gone on strike until they have better conditions."

Lord Sinclair almost fell to the ground. How could they do this at such a time? Although, on one hand he admired their choice of timing. He knew that they knew that they had him exactly where they wanted.

"What are their demands?" asked Lord Sinclair.

"They want one day off every two weeks, a separate blanket and a stack of hay so that when they sleep on the floors they are more comfortable, and an extra coin or two in their pay," said the Head of his Household.

Lord Sinclair was paralysed unsure what to do. Can he really negotiate changes to the Royal Household without discussing it with the King? He thought it was best to seek his approval. He therefore gestured that he will be back and headed upstairs to the banqueting hall.

He went to the King and asked for a quick word, crouching down beside him.

"Sinclair, when is the food? I am peckish and all this excitement has my stomach rumbling like the storms of Scotland that sank the Spanish Armada!" asked the King in a jovial mood.

"There is a slight issue with that. The servants from your Royal Household who are supporting today have gone on strike seeking better conditions," explained Lord Sinclair nervously.

"What?" said the King, his demeanour completely changing to one of indignation of how these lowly servants can question him. "Listen Sinclair, just sort it. I don't care about the details - just don't be too generous."

And with that Lord Sinclair went back downstairs to begin the negotiations.

"Ok, here's the deal. The King isn't impressed but will provide separate blankets and hay to aid sleeping, but that's it. And he won't be held to ransom."

The Head of Household listened and gathered the servants in a huddle. They spoke amongst themselves for a couple of minutes. Lord Sinclair struggled to hear exactly what was said. Eventually he made his way back to Lord Sinclair.

"No," said the Head of the Household.

"What do you mean by no?" asked Lord Sinclair who was flabbergasted.

"They say no. No deal."

"What's their counter proposal?"

"There is no counter proposal. They want the day off, the comfort and the extra pay."

"I can't do that."

"Well, I'm sorry Sir, but they can't work."

Lord Sinclair mused at this development stroking his chin thoughtfully.

"Ok, it's a deal. They can have what they asked for."

The rest of the kitchen had heard that and there were cheers amongst the servants. Lord Sinclair headed back upstairs and went to the King.

"Excellent news, your Majesty," began Lord Sinclair. "I've got them back to work. All it took was a day off every couple of weeks, some blankets and hay for their sleeping arrangements, and an extra coin or two in their pay."

"Well done, Sinclair. I knew you'd solve it," said the King pleased with Lord Sinclair's negotiation skills.

Lord Sinclair wiped the sweat away from his brow realising that he had bluffed the King and survived. Time to enjoy the meal.

The servants then brought the food in on platters. It was quite a sight with servant after servant bringing in silver trays stuffed full of patisseries, fruit, sugar and sugared fruit preserves. It was all the rage to have sugar hits as a sign of wealth. Sugar was a rare commodity, and this was an excessive display of wealth.

The silver trays were placed one between two for people to share - the mess, as it was called was quite generous as it wasn't unusual for an entire family to share one mess. This was Lord Sinclair's event, so he was keen to show his wealth to others including the boastful Lord Maitland. So, one mess between two was a statement. The King had his own mess as is standard.

One of the silver trays had the most prized items, fruit. Pears to be more precise. This was too precious to be contained in the mess so instead had its own silver tray. Fresh fruit couldn't be preserved and had to be eaten relatively quickly so it was very rare. Pears were the order of the day and a nod to the King, given that Queen Mary's favourite fruit was pears. This platter was placed closest to the King as a sign of respect. It would have been inappropriate to have the most expensive item at the wrong end of the table.

The combination of wine that kept flowing and sugar that was being digested created a lively dim of conversation, laughter, and drunken shouting.

The King chomped on the pears eating six of the eight on the platter before gesturing that others could have it. The Ambassador sprightly leapt from the bench at the other end of the table and took one of the two remaining pears. Nobody had seen him move so quickly for at least 20 years. There was one pear left and with Lord Sinclair on one side of the King and Lord Maitland on the other, it was a battle of wills as to who would take the final remaining pear. Both looked at each other. Lord Maitland stood up and picked up the silver tray, but instead of taking it for himself he passed it over to Lord Sinclair and gestured for him to take it. He did and thanked Lord Maitland for the offer. It was very civil despite their natural jockeying for a position with the King. Lord Sinclair saw the gesture through a negative lens. He deemed it to be a clever move on Lord Maitland's part to appear humble and collaborative in front of the King. He was sure that if the King wasn't there that Lord Maitland would have thrown it in the fireplace ahead of handing him that precious pear. Lord Sinclair relaxed and quietened down when he started eating the pear given how succulent and juicy it was.

As everyone was almost finished and there was little left in the mess, Lord Sinclair motioned to one servant. They immediately blew out all the candles without warning. William then stood up and went to the front of the table in front of everyone, although they could barely see him and he then boomed his voice across the room.

"May I now invite you to the start of the Masque. Queen Anne of Denmark has arranged for one of the most sought after performers in all of Northern Europe to be present here this evening. He has been in France, Denmark, the German Republic and is now here in Aberdeenshire. May I present *The Moore?*"

Polite applause followed. Then in the shadows, a performer appeared with his body gyrating gracefully from left to right, from up to down, from right to left. He or she was a beautifully graceful performer. Gliding like a swan, a ballerina and a poet rolled up into one. Lady Maitland cried as the musician's accompanying music suited perfectly the Moore's movements.

There seemed to be some story to his movements. The music started off sad and his movements echoed the cold beauty of a frozen winter landscape. Later on, his movements were joyful reminiscence of a warm summer's day. It was as if it was a tale of two seasons.

The servants then lit a few more of the candles to coincide with the joyful portion of the performance. The movements became more energetic and more frenzied. Like something that nobody had seen before. It was not European. It was violent, it was passionate. Lady Maitland wasn't crying but was in a state of ecstasy as the crescendo built. The Ambassador had been all over the world but he had seen nothing like it. The poets, William and Mark were transfixed on the performer's movements. It was a man who was putting on this powerful performance. Lord Sinclair and Lord Maitland were intrigued. Andrew and Jane Melville felt out of place never seeing such entertainment, and Lady Sinclair was stroking her husband's hands in a way he hadn't seen for quite a while.

Eventually, the crescendo reached its natural peak with the music frenzied as well and then all of a sudden the performer jumped ten feet in the air and landed perfectly just as the servants had lit all the candles and the room was at full brightness again. Everyone gasped. The Moore was a man clearly from Africa. Nobody, not even the King, had seen a man from Africa before. His moves were things nobody had seen before. There was a stunned silence in the room but then the King quickly stood and applauded wildly. Everyone followed cheering and whooping. The Moore had been an incredible hit. What a superstar. What a gift that Queen Anne had given to her fiancé. It was a complete honour for everyone in the room to have seen that performance.

The Moore didn't hang around for the crowd to cheer too long before he continued into his second performance. This was turning into a very memorable masque. A masque was a theatrical show and entertainment that took place in Courts of the time so the King was well accustomed to seeing many varying quality of masques but this was shaping up to be a very memorable performance.

The Moore was now on all fours and joined by an exotic indigenous woman. She looked of New World origins. The Moore had a loin cloth and what appeared to be golden chains with the indigenous woman wearing a tight cloth that barely covered her breasts and waist. They were both stunningly gorgeous. The Moore was now pretending to be a lion moving menacingly around the room and table - growling and owning the room as if he were the most powerful thing in there. Everyone had forgotten about the King's powers during this performance, such was the strength of the movement. The indigenous woman was following him as if she was controlling the chains that kept the lion from escaping but when she moved, the men's eyes were drawn to her. The Moore paused at Lady Maitland and looked at her. Fear and excitement at the same time was all over her face. He pawed her. Her joy seemed to increase. Then without warning, the Moore ran away off the table and out of the room with the indigenous woman close behind him.

The performance was over. The room stood applauding wildly, cheering, gasping. It was a gift from Queen Anne that nobody would forget.

"I think I might need to lie down after that," bellowed the King.

The Moore then came back into the room normally dressed. Everyone immediately quietened to see what would happen next. He stood at the end of the table and began.

"Blessed are all who fear the Lord, who walk in his ways. You will eat the fruit of your labour; blessings and prosperity will be yours. Your wife will be like a fruitful vine within your house; your sons will be like olive shoots around your table. Thus is the man blessed who fears the Lord."

He had just quoted Psalm 128.

"You must eat with us, sit here next to Lady Maitland," instructed the King.

This was unusual but everyone was excited to be joined by the Moore. Lord Sinclair had a smirk on his face. Everyone had seen how much Lady Maitland had enjoyed the performance so him being sat next to her was sure to agitate Lord Maitland.

But before the Moore could take a seat, he had one last thing to do. He disappeared for a moment and then came back gracefully holding the centrepiece for dinner. It was an enlarged model of a ship but it was stuffed with different fish; herring, flounders, whiting, oysters, whelks, crabs, and clams. It was an extravaganza of fish - all seasoned with sugar. This really was a luxury meal. After gliding across the room and placing the centrepiece at the middle of the table, the Moore then sat down next to Lady Maitland, which made her giggle.

Servants brought the rest of the meal. Besides fish, there were messes full of salads, leeks, onions, radishes, cabbage, lettuce, chives, boiled carrots, flowers, and herbs. They were all in oil with vinegar and a sugar dressing.

Everybody ate after the King took his first bite, and the meal was being pleasantly enjoyed by all. It was just incredibly sweet which led Andrew to ask, "what's with all this sugar?"

"Andrew, my boy, you don't realise do you?" replied Lord Sinclair.

"No, I'm afraid not,"

"Well, sugar as I'm sure you are aware is a very expensive ingredient. It means that only the wealthy can afford it. It is only used for occasions such as this. Also, this is all the rage in Italy now. It's the Italian way to drape everything in sugar. Yes, there is a lot of French influence here but sometimes we like to extend as far as Venice!" replied Lord Sinclair.

Lord Sinclair then picked up one quaiche containing sweet wine that was poured as a meal accompaniment. He clinked it and said, "You see this Andrew? This is Venetian. A Venetian sweet wine, Italian influenced meal. We are the global elite."

And with that he got back to enjoying the meal. It seemed to make sense to Andrew, so he too got back to chomping the crab that lay on his mess.

The meal went on for quite some time as all the guests

gorged on the fresh cuts of fish. Spirits were in good stead helping by the sugar and sweet wine.

Eventually, all the messes were empty. The silver platter was only a distant memory of what it contained. The guests dispersed from the table and moved to different areas of the banqueting hall.

Lord Sinclair, Lord Maitland, and the Ambassador were deep in conversation at one end.

"I still can't believe that the King forced us into financing this English Armada," said an exasperated Lord Maitland.

"Agreed. I look at the Ambassador when he told us to invest in Muscovy shares and how much money we made," said Lord Sinclair whilst putting a friendly arm around the Ambassador, "and then I look at the worthless pieces of paper we have from our investment in the English Armada Joint Stock Company and despair."

"I have an idea," said Lord Maitland. "Do you have your shares somewhere here?"

"Yes, I do."

"Bring them to me."

And with that Lord Sinclair disappeared off to his study on the top floor. He had to rummage around quite a few papers before he found it. There it was, the English Armada Joint Stock Company. A nice ship motif was watermarked in the background with a Royal seal on the front. It looked quite regal. He headed back downstairs and handed it to Lord Maitland.

Lord Maitland then made his way to the Moore who was in deep discussion with the Ladies and the Melville's.

"Moore, I was so impressed with your performance tonight that I wanted to give you a personal gift." began Lord Maitland. "I have in my hand, a certificate for shares in a Joint Stock Company. Do you know what a Joint Stock Company is?"

The Moore didn't, so he nodded his head to signify no - but he could tell this was an important piece of paper.

"Well, this piece of paper means that the holder of it owns 1% of the English Armada. Given that there were 150 ships, this means that the holder of this piece of paper owns 1 and a half ships. The ships, the crew and, more importantly, everything that the ship brings from abroad. That all goes to the holder of this piece of paper."

"That is impressive. I didn't know that a piece of paper could do that," said the Moore.

"It can, and guess what, this piece of paper is now yours. My gift to you for your magical performance." And with that, Lord Maitland handed the Moore the piece of paper.

The Moore looked at it in disbelief. He had performed all over Europe and was from a humble African background - and he now owned 1 and a half ships! Not any ships, but English ships! Everybody across the world knew that the English had the strongest navy.

"I thank-you enormously, kind sir." said the Moore before bowing in appreciation.

And with that, Lord Maitland made his way back to Lord Sinclair and the Ambassador. He turned to have a look around him and he could see all the group studying closely the impressive piece of paper that the Moore now had in his possession.

"You are incredibly cruel, Maitland," said Lord Sinclair.

"I don't know. The Moore now owns one and a half ships of the Queen's navy," chipped in the Ambassador.

"Shame they are at the bottom of the Bay of Corunna!" bellowed Lord Maitland. And with that, they all shared a laugh at the Moore's expense.

"Instead of trying to invade Europe, we should start a plantation in Ulster," said the Ambassador.

"I thought you were trying to get funding to go to the New World?" enquired Lord Maitland.

"Why? Are you interested now?" quipped the Ambassador, not missing any opportunity to push his idea.

"Definitely not," confirmed Lord Maitland.

Ulster on the island of Ireland was beautiful. Green rolling hills, very few towns or villages. It was a picturesque beauty. A throwback to yesteryear with rural life dominating the region. It was as Gaelic as you can imagine. There weren't any English or Scottish influences and was an unfamiliar world. It was therefore an opportunity that a few of the Lords had suggested to King James, and now the Ambassador was doing the same. Ulster was seen as an undeveloped and underpopulated area ripe for agricultural farmlands. The locals were nomadic moving their flock in the summer months to uplands before sheltering in the winter. They were simple people. The English had various battles over the years to bring order to this region but it wasn't a sustained effort to take control.

"You know, Ambassador, you are right. These exotic adventures are too expensive and too risky. We just need to bring some order and culture to create a civilisation in Ulster. They are just barbarians on the island. A bit of Scottish discipline will set them right. All they need is some good Protestant values in their souls." said Lord Sinclair.

"Good - will you please raise this with the King?" asked the Ambassador.

"Have you forgotten that the English frequently have battles with the Irish? If we were to go in heavy handed, we'd start a war with the English! The farmers will get taken care of but we need to manage the situation carefully," replied Lord Sinclair.

The King had now joined the group that contained the Moore and a loud laugh could be heard from across the room.

The King then bellowed, "Maitland, you are one cruel fellow!"

Some further words were exchanged between the King and the Moore. A look of disappointment had reached his face. He probably knew his ships were at the bottom of the ocean and not full of gold returning from some conquest overseas.

The King had now hobbled his way over to join their group.

"Oh Maitland, you are a comedian. I know all of you are disappointed by the English Armada but look at it as an investment. By supporting Elizabeth, we've sent a message that we are one union. When I take the power of both lands, we will have our dividends and you know that I will look after you." said the King.

"Thank-you your Majesty. I had a question for you, when you become ruler of both lands - where will your base be?" enquired Lord Maitland.

"Scotland is in my bones," confirmed the King. "Whilst I may have to set up base in London as that is where all the money and decisions are made believe me that I live for Scotland. The highlands, the fresh Scottish air. This is my home. This is the land that God gave me to govern. God has in his plans for me to be like Banquo and inherit England too but Scotland will always have a special place in my heart."

"We will see, your Majesty," said Lord Maitland. "I can see you really enjoying London and in particular the Tower of London. What Henry VII setup is a joy to behold. You won't believe the exotic menagerie that is housed there. I've seen polar bears, lions, and elephants. Can you believe it? In London!"

King James swung his hand dismissively as if to say, don't be silly, but you could see in his eyes that he was intrigued by this animal prison in the Tower of London. The King was an animal lover, but it was more towards viewing animals as there for Man's pleasure and entertainment. The King didn't view animal cruelty as anything to be concerned about.

And with that, they all raised a glass, "To Scotland", they all said before bumping their quaiches and taking a swig of sweet wine.

"Sinclair, I need a word with you," said the King.

The two of them moved a few feet away.

"I have a request. That indigenous woman that performed with the Moore. You know which one?" asked the King.

"Of course, I couldn't forget her performance," confirmed Lord Sinclair.

"Have her waiting in my bedchamber within 5 minutes," asked the King.

Lord Sinclair was slightly surprised by the request but agreed. He went to whisper to a servant and then left the room.

The King returned to Lord Maitland and the Ambassador.

"So Ambassador how was your journey from London?" asked the King.

"It was fine," confirmed the Ambassador. "But I met a strange young man when I reached York. My carriage had stopped to replenish supplies and there was a young man in a similar position and we started talking. He was around 18 years old and had told me his life story about how his father died when he was just a boy and he inherited this big estate just outside York. He was planning to sell it so he could go off to Europe to fight for the Catholics and kept going on about how the Catholic faith was the only way to gain redemption on this earth. Eventually the conversation moved on to Mary and the Bible. He seemed like a bit of a maniac to me, and had a strange name, Guido or something."

"Guido, with a name like that he ought to make candles - not fighting wars!" joked the King.

"He was a strange fellow, believe me."

"He sounds like a viper. To sell his Father's estate to fight for the Catholics is unacceptable." said the King in a harsh tone.

The King then made his way to his bedchamber. The indigenous woman was standing there dressed like somewhere between a servant and a lady. Not as lowly as a servant but nowhere near the levels of a sophisticated lady. She was 5 foot 2 with a small face with short black hair scrunched in a pony tail. Her face looked exotic with her big juicy lips. Her body was taut for someone who danced for several hours a day. Her legs toned and shimmering in the candle light.

The King sat on the bed whilst the woman remained in the centre.

"Take off your clothes," said the King.

The woman did nothing. She remained stood still. She didn't understand what the King had said, so he repeated.

"Take off your clothes."

She still didn't understand his words, but she understood the look in his eyes. It was a look that she had seen many times before from men. And with that, she removed her clothes and let them fall to the floor. She was now naked and ambled towards him. She had experienced this many times with wealthy men and those of power, but never with a King. And never with a King that had a reputation that would have made such an encounter seem unlikely.

The King pulled her to him and then took what he wanted.

CHAPTER EIGHT

T he post banquet celebrations were now in full swing. The King had returned from spending some time upstairs and some guests were getting more rowdy. Lady Maitland who so enjoyed the Moore's performance was dancing and her attempts to get a dance partner were failing so far. The Moore had been a particular target of hers but he was smart enough to know that dancing in public with a powerful man's wife, even if he had been made fun of with his naval ships gift, was unwise and would probably have ended with him in prison or worse.

She therefore made a beeline for the Ambassador. Her enthusiasm clear for all to see.

"Ambassador, come and dance with me," begged Lady Maitland.

"My dear," responded the Ambassador. "I am an old man who has difficulty walking. I would like nothing more than to dance with you, but I fear my dancing days are long behind me."

"Ok, how about we talk for a little while?" asked Lady Maitland.

"Of course," said the Ambassador, more than happy for

a beautiful woman's company.

They then sat down on one bench. The Ambassador slowly lowered himself to take a seat, whilst Lady Maitland sat on his side with her hand gently resting on his knee.

"You have led such an incredible life," began Lady Maitland. "I look at you with nothing but admiration. I fear that Lord Maitland may one day discard me like a piece of fruit discarded by the King once he has finished feasting," shared a thoughtful Lady Maitland.

"My dear, he will never discard you. You are every man's dream. My life has been perhaps more complicated than others, but time finds everyone. My ideas are not worth what they once were."

"Nonsense, Ambassador! You live in London, you've been to the German Republic, Russia, and France. The wealth you must have amassed over the years on those journeys. I hear how my husband talks about all the wealth you've created to everyone through the Muscovy company."

"My dear. I am but a humble civil servant employed by either the court of the Queen of England or the court of the King of Scotland. I have no vast wealth, no shares in Muscovy. I did my job, which was to serve the Country and am proud for having done so."

Lady Maitland was taken aback by this. For someone as important and worldly as the Ambassador not to have amassed any wealth at his age was unbelievable, but perhaps it was making sense. Maybe this is why her husband and Lord Sinclair would mock the Ambassador. Maybe they had little respect for a man who didn't grease his own palm a little whilst making everyone else rich. And now here he was reduced to plugging his latest investment opportunity and receiving scorn from ungrateful people who he had made rich several years earlier. The world was a brutal place. These thoughts were depressing Lady Maitland, so she thanked the Ambassador for the talk and then got back up to dance away back into the crowd to lift her spirits back to a party mood.

And so the party continued, with different groups mingling. People dancing. Drinks being consumed. General merriment was being had. That was until there was a crashing sound on the ceiling. It was loud enough to have the musicians stop playing their instruments. The conversation in the room suddenly quietened to silence. Even Lady Maitland eventually stopped dancing when she had realised what had happened.

It was an odd sound, so the guests investigated what the sound was. Lord Sinclair led the way but assured everyone that he was sure it was fine. As they made their way up the stairs, Lord Sinclair encountered a servant who was heading downstairs to tell him the news.

"Claude has returned," exclaimed the servant.

"Well, that is fantastic!" said an excited Lord Sinclair.

"Who on earth is this Claude?" asked the King.

Lord Sinclair then told the story, "I have a dovecot as I am a huge bird lover. I find them to be magnificent creatures. They are intelligent, loyal, and calm. Qualities I look for in a man, let alone fowl. Claude was an exquisite carrier pigeon that I gained in a game of Noddy. Claude was sent to France several months ago to deliver a message to a business contact. He has now returned."

Homing pigeons carrying messages were used for centuries with the Romans using birds to deliver messages to the front line in battles and the Greeks using them in the Olympics so they really were nothing new. However, that communication channel was now under threat from Franz Von Taxis who had set up a network of horse couriers across Western Europe. Something that the English had copied. It was with this knowledge that the expectations placed on homing birds had increased.

"After several months? That's unacceptable. I could have had a servant return within several weeks," said an unimpressed King.

It was then that events took an odd turn. The King instructed Lord Sinclair to take him to the dovecot to show him Claude. The King and all the guests followed Lord Sinclair to the dovecot. It was smelly and there were already three other birds in the tiny nest like house. Lord Sinclair reached in and pulled out Claude, handing him to the King. Claude was white with his feathers glistening in the candle light. The King didn't know too much about pigeons, but it didn't take an expert to know that this was no ordinary bird. It looked like one of the King's pedigree horses, a topic he knew a lot about.

"Now," began the King. "Claude has failed as a carrier pigeon. This is unacceptable. If he was on business for Lord Sinclair, then that means he was on business for the land of Scotland. The land of Scotland is my duty to protect and as God has put me on this earth to protect it, then, so I will. Claude will have to prove his worth to survive. Claude will have to survive one minute in a pan of boiling water. If he does so, then he will be set free."

The guests gasped. Lord Sinclair's face had dropped.

This was cruelty of the highest order. This wouldn't be a test, but just torture of an innocent bird. It was known that the King had some strange hobbies, but he had sank to a new low.

The guests prepared to make their ways to the Kitchens to see this odd and cruel form of entertainment. The King hobbled his way down the stairs but he caught his foot in one of the cracks and had to let go of the bird to stop himself falling flat on his face. He averted injury by clinging to the wall. That was a successful escape. However, Claude too had a successful escape and had flown away out of the Castle, probably sensing that remaining here would have been unwise.

Lord Sinclair tried to stifle his smirk, but he couldn't and a slight smile crept along his face. Luckily the King was further behind so didn't see this.

The King, not wanting to lose respect, proclaimed, "God has spoken. I have pardoned Claude. He is now free instead. A King can be cruel and kind. You can all see how kind your King is. Now, everyone back to the party. This is a celebration, after all!"

Everyone went back downstairs to the banqueting hall in much better spirits than they were a few seconds earlier, but they were all a little taken aback by the recent events.

There were servants there waiting for them with tankards of ale. It wasn't a drink that Lady Maitland or Lady Sinclair particularly enjoyed but they were repulsed by what they were almost close to witnessing so they took the ale and promptly drank almost half of what was in the tankard. This would help them forget what had just happened, at least that was what they hoped.

Andrew was in conversation with the Ambassador. He was still thinking about the mental anguish that Jane was going through thanks to the witches curse. He broached the subject with the Ambassador.

"Ambassador, I have a delicate matter that I want to discuss with you but I ask that you keep it in the utmost secrecy," said Andrew.

"Spit it out," replied an intrigued Ambassador.

"Well, Jane is in a panic because a witch placed a curse on her. We haven't told the King because we fear for what he might do,"

"I see your predicament. Have you heard of *Mallesus Maleficarum*?" asked the Ambassador.

"No I haven't."

"Well, it's the book on witchcraft. How to detect it and how to eradicate it. Written by two Germans, I believe. I read it maybe 40 years ago, so my mind is a bit hazy. The first part tells you all about why you should fear them, so best to skip that. The second part was about some sins that witches have done such as entering into sexual relations with devils and their night flights, scary stuff. The last part was all about the legal actions that you can take. Torturing to gain confessions is ok. This book has been endorsed by both Protestants and Catholics. This is the real deal - get it."

"Legal action? Can't I place a counter spell?" asked Andrew.

The Ambassador got really agitated.

"What are you trying to do to me? Talking about placing spells on people in public! In fact, don't mention that to me, even in private. Only witches place spells. The best thing that you can hope for is to start legal action, we'll get her tortured and then she'll end up thrown in the river. If she floats then we'll know she is a witch and we'll burn her at the stake. If she drowns then you'll have peace of mind because you'll know she was just a crackpot."

"Thanks Ambassador, that makes perfect sense," said Andrew profusely shaking the Ambassador's hands.

Elsewhere in the hall, the poets Mark and William were together in one corner and it was quite a sight. They were laughing wildly, delicately grasping one another by the shoulders. You could see two people who were very comfortable in each other's presence and had genuine affection for one another. The King from across the room had an envious look in his eyes, so when Mark left William to go to the toilet, the King followed him. After Mark had finished using the toilet, the King bumped into him.

"Sorry, didn't see you there," said the King. "Could you come to my bedchamber to talk and hug?"

"Of course," replied Mark.

Mark followed the King to his bedchamber, which was candlelit given that it was now late into the evening. The night sky was calm, and the stars shone through the windows, adding an extra illumination into the room.

Mark took some tobacco out of his pocket and filled his pipe before lighting it. The King looked on, astonished. Everybody knew that the King hated smoking, but

Mark either had forgotten or did it as a provocative act. The answer quickly came when he blew a smoke ring toward the King, which riled the King.

"Why must you smoke? Don't you realise the damage you are doing?" asked the King.

"I'm really dirty, am I not? This filthy smoke just oozing out of me. Send me away to keep your Majesty untarnished from my filthy self."

But the King would not send Mark away. He found this provocative behaviour both exhilarating and disgusting at the same time.

"Do you not feel ashamed? You don't realise the damage you are doing to your lungs and yourself. Equally, by my presence being here, you are also hurting my lungs and myself. It's also a sin against God to harm one's body."

Mark looked at the King and took another puff, "You believe in witches, mystic potions, and your divine right to rule all of Scotland and England. You believe that one of man's great pleasures, a crop that has been smoked for as long as Man has been alive on this earth to be toxic. If that were the case, then Man would no longer be on this earth. Next you will tell me that pleasures of the human body are a sin too?"

"Don't take witches lightly, Mark," said the King. "I don't want you to just believe in their power but to really lead the charge against them. What they are doing is high treason against God. And don't forget it's not just witches but vampires, werewolves, and unicorns are amongst us as well. The actual danger is that females are easily influenced by witches. That is why I much prefer the company of men, where possible."

Mark wanted to change the subject, so he just took a puff and blew another smoke ring towards the window.

This didn't impress the King, "Smoking is hateful to the nose. Just smell your clothes, your lips."

"Why don't you come here and smell my lips?" asked Mark.

The King was so annoyed with Mark, but yet he couldn't tear himself away. Mark was exotic and French - a combination that the King couldn't ignore. That Mark smoked and was also a Catholic meant he was the forbidden fruit, and Mark knew it.

The King leaned over to kiss Mark and just before their lips met, Mark blew a smoke ring in the King's face and then laughed hysterically.

This annoyed the King, "You are such an immature child. You never think about the deep topics that concern mankind. You never think about why we are on this earth and you behave like an immature child in the most sensitive and inappropriate moments."

Now, this was a small wake up call for Mark. For all his bravado, he liked the King's attention and could feel it slipping away. He stubbed out his tobacco, and then turned to the King.

"I'm sorry, let's discuss something deep and thoughtful, what do you want to discuss?" said a rueful Mark.

"Let me share with you what I've recently been thinking about, my time on the English throne will come soon. The role of the government is therefore on my mind. I view it split into three parts. First, my duty is to be a good Christian to God. I love and respect God - but I also fear him. I want you to be a good Christian too. You need to study both the old and new testament. Pray often and be grateful for what you have."

"I will try," replied Mark. "I think about my role on earth. I know I seem casual at times but the life of a poet is full of laughter and adventures - but I wouldn't be able to write the poetry that I do if I didn't have moments of contemplation. I will try to become closer to God for you."

"You need to become closer to God for yourself, Mark, not for me," replied the King. "But it's a step in the right direction. The second key part of governing is to not be a tyrant. I want to ensure we have laws established and executed that are fair and just. I will visit each of my kingdom's every three years as they need to know that I care."

"Do you really see your head not being turned by the bright lights of London?" asked Mark.

"Lord Maitland asked me the same thing. It is interesting that you all don't understand that Kingship is a duty bestowed on me by God. I am not a mere mortal whose head will be turned by the lights of London. The other key part of not being a tyrant is to understand mathematics for military purposes and world history for foreign policy. That is why I encourage foreign merchants to come here and why we use Gold and Silver as currency. It has to be a lesson from history."

"Tell me more, King, you are so wise and passionate when you speak," chipped in Mark admiringly.

"My heir will have everything. I have seen so many squabbles between family members on what is left that I will not place my family and my people in that predicament. My heir shall inherit everything. The last piece that I was thinking about is the daily life of a monarch."

"Daily life? You mean such as going to the bakery and washing?" asked Mark, displaying his simple background to the King.

"Not quite, Mark, although you are on the right track. Eating properly is important as that creates energy. Drinking too much and sleeping too much are out too."

Mark thought to himself that the King might take some of his own advice regarding drinking. The King then continued, "Appearance is important; always to be clean and never allow one's nails or hair to get too long. Honesty and clarity in language is important too."

"That's one thing I can identify with," chipped in Mark wanting to show how they were alike, when it was clear they were nothing of the sort.

"I enjoy talking with you," said the King. He then kissed Mark on the cheek and headed back downstairs.

CHAPTER NINE

L ord Sinclair was in a much more relaxed mood. The banquet was a hit, and his hosting skills had been admired by all. The King approached him and they sat next to each other on one bench.

"Sinclair, you've done a fine job," began the King.

"Thank-you, your majesty," replied a beaming Lord Sinclair.

"This evening has really clicked for me," said the King. "I enjoyed the Moore's performance so much. This theatrical performance or masque, as I prefer them to be called, will be the centrepiece of our foreign entertaining going forwards. We will wow the world with our ability to put on a masque. However, we need a venue fit for such an event. I'm thinking we will need the English purse to build this cathedral for entertainment that I have envisioned. It will be the grandest hall in all of Europe to marvel and delight visitors for centuries to come; exotic in style but with Scotland at its heart. It will cost a fortune and be a statement of our power as a nation!"

This astonished Lord Sinclair, he was glad that the evening had made such an impression on the King, but he wasn't finished yet.

"Sinclair, my banqueting hall will be classical in concept with a refined Italianate Renaissance style coupled with the picturesque beauty of Jacobean architecture. And Flemish Mannerists! That is what it needs as well."

Lord Sinclair started laughing. He did not understand what the King said, but he could see that he was happy. The King joined in the laughter and the two friends were in that perfect state of bliss for a second without a care in the world.

"Your castle is fantastic, real homely," said the King.

"Thank-you, that is the highest compliment you could have given," said Lord Sinclair.

"I tell you, the other thing you don't have, which you need, is a golf course. How can a gentleman not have their own private golf course? It's no wonder that you never win when we play," said the King.

Lord Sinclair thought he won half of the time when they played. The difference being that he would pay when he lost whereas the King never did, hence why he never recalled losing to Lord Sinclair.

"I think that is a wise suggestion. I would like a golf course but alas my family fear I will be on the course all the time," said Lord Sinclair.

"You are right, Sinclair, wise move not to have one under your nose," replied the King.

An odd event was happening a few metres away. The rest of the guests were split into two and it looked as if an impromptu performance was taking place. The King and Lord Sinclair were keen to ensure that they didn't miss out, so paid close attention to the events unfolding in front of their eyes.

Mark and William were on opposite sides with long loaves of bread used as mock swords. Lady Maitland and the Moore were on Mark's team, following him around as he charged at William. William had Lady Sinclair and Jane Melville retreating alongside him as he defended himself from the charging Mark.

"Take that! You Spanish swine," shouted Mark.

"You shall eat your own bread, you pompous English man," shouted William back.

"We shall defeat you again like we defeated you on the coast of Scotland," bellowed Mark as he thrust his loaf of bread towards William's group. The bread shed some crumbs as he thrust it forward.

"No! You will be defeated like we sunk your famed English Armada," responded William, dodging the loaf of bread.

Suddenly, the loaf of bread struck Jane Melville - who became the first casualty in this reconstruction of the ongoing English - Spanish war.

The King thought how ridiculous this entire war was. The loaves of bread had the scene looking more fanciful, but with a serious undertone behind it. As the King went to pick up Jane Melville, he said to her, "Looks like your luck has gone against you."

"I beg your pardon?" said a worried looking Jane.

"I said that your luck has gone against you, the first casualty of the English-Spanish war," clarified the King, smiling widely.

Jane was still sensitive about the witch that turned up unannounced and had placed a curse on her, all for supporting the King who was now standing in front of her eyes. She wanted to tell him to get a reassuring word or some kind of counter spell from one of the King's favoured spirit communicators, but she feared how he would respond. She therefore let out a fake laugh and got back to the mock war.

It was now into the early hours of the night, and guests were tiring. The Ambassador was the first to go to sleep. He did so with no big proclamation. He just headed upstairs. In fact, nobody noticed. They only realised that he had gone to sleep when Lord Maitland wanted to make another joke at the Ambassador's expense. This acted as a trigger for Andrew & Jane, who also retired for the night. They were used to waking up early to ensure that breakfast was prepared correctly for their Royal masters, so staying up so late was a very rare occurrence. Jane would have a difficult night's sleep due to the stresses caused from worrying about the curse.

The Poets were still in full voice and humour. They were speaking French, German, Dutch, and it all sounded so poetic. One was standing, and the other was jumping, and then they took turns and swapped. The King with all of his aches and illnesses looked at them with awe and a tinge of jealousy.

Lady Maitland was in one corner in deep conversation with the Moore. It was difficult to tell exactly what was being said, but Lord Maitland was paying close attention to them.

Lord Sinclair was feeling tired. The stresses of the event had died down, and the Adrenalin had dissipated, leaving him both physically and mentally shattered. Lady Sinclair put her arm around him and said, "Why don't you go to bed?"

"I can't. I'm the host. How will it look?" asked Lord Sinclair.

"Just ask the King. Look at him. He looks like he is ready to end the night too," observed Lady Sinclair.

"You are right."

And with that Lord Sinclair approached the King, asking to go to sleep.

"Excellent idea, Sinclair. It's been a long night," replied the King.

And with that the King loudly gave his good night wishes to nobody in particular to signify the end of the evening. That gave Lord Sinclair the freedom to go to sleep.

That left the last revellers being the poets Mark and William, Lord & Lady Maitland, Lady Sinclair, and the Moore.

Lord Maitland wasn't too pleased with the Moore still being here. It was now inappropriate given that the King had left, and the host had left too.

"Moore - time for you to go downstairs to the cold Kitchen floor," instructed Lord Maitland.

The Moore stopped his conversation with Lady Maitland, turned and looked at Lord Maitland. A thousand thoughts raced through his mind. The justice of life. The consequences of actions. The options he had. But he settled for the sensible one.

"It's been a long night. Good night everyone," said the Moore, heading downstairs to that cold Kitchen floor.

"If it's time for the artists to go, then we'll bid you farewell," said Mark. Mark and William then immediately disappeared, not waiting for any confirmation. They didn't want to hang around this crowd as it bored them so headed upstairs but instead of going to their bedchamber, they opened the door to the master bedchamber where the King was now sleeping.

Mark entered one side of the bed, and William entered another side. The King was still snoring and had barely moved. They both sniggered as the King looked very normal, and actually a little repulsive. William hugged the King from one, and Mark from the other. Mark's arm was stroking William's. The King remained in a state of drunkenness and continued to snore away. It looked like the King's adventures for the evening were at an end.

Back in the banqueting hall, Lord Maitland was looking at Lady Sinclair with an inquisitive eye.

"Tell me, Lady Sinclair, when was the last time your husband made love to you?" asked Lord Maitland.

Lady Sinclair immediately blushed and pretended to be offended, but she appreciated what she interpreted to be interest. Lady Maitland was sat next to Lord Maitland during all of this and kept her smile throughout. She wasn't surprised by the question.

"Well, I don't know. I don't quite remember, but I don't want to discuss this with you," replied Lady Sinclair.

"You really are beautiful," said Lady Maitland.

Lady Sinclair quickly realising that Lady Maitland was a more carefree character than even she thought possible, wondering where this was all headed. She knew that Lord Sinclair had run-ins with Lord Maitland and they were constantly trying to outdo each other so was wary of being a pawn in some petty minor feud.

"I think it's getting late," said Lady Sinclair, feigning a yawn.

"I agree," said Lord Maitland. "You know, your husband looked exhausted tonight. It is very stressful to host such an event. Why don't you just let him sleep in his bedchamber? Don't disturb him. He is a wonderful man and deserves some rest."

"And where would I sleep?" asked Lady Sinclair, although she had an inkling of what the answer might be.

"With us," said Lady Maitland immediately. Her beautiful smile invitingly beckoning her.

"I'm sorry. I must go," replied Lady Sinclair. And with that she ran out of the banqueting hall and up the stairs straight to her husband. She ran into the room at such a pace that she woke him up.

"Are you ok dear?" asked Lord Sinclair.

"Sorry to have woken you. Yes, I'm fine. The party has ended now, and everyone has gone to sleep. I think sugar has a very energetic quality to it, as I didn't even realise that I was running. Sorry again to have woken you. Go back to sleep."

And with that, she stroked Lord Sinclair's cheek and then got into bed alongside him.

Lord and Lady Maitland had also gone to bed, laughing as they made their way upstairs. Lady Sinclair heard this and wondered whether that had just been a prank and what would have happened if she had said yes to join them. She would never know and eventually fell asleep, despite the excess amount of sugar. All the guests did. The excitement of the night, the activities, all of it. It has been a memorable evening, and they were all exhausted. They all fell asleep, and the Castle was quiet - except for the King's snoring. Claude had also returned to his dovecot knowing that nobody was after him any longer.

CHAPTER TEN

Everyone was fast asleep, and it was now well into the early hours. The sky was still and the night sky at its darkest. This peace however, was about to be shattered. A visitor was fast arriving on a horse galloping across the horizon. Eventually the visitor arrived and barely secured his horse before he pounded strongly on the door with his fist. He also started shouting, "Lord Sinclair, wake up. I must speak with you."

This commotion awoke the servants on the lower levels, and the Head of the Household gingerly made his way to the door and opened it.

"I must see Lord Sinclair at once," announced the stranger.

"I don't think you understand. What is your name?" replied the Head of the Household.

"I'm the Earl of Bothwell," replied the stranger and with that he pushed past the Head of the Household and made his way up the stairs.

The Earl of Bothwell, not to be confused with Lord Bothwell who was the previous holder of the title and his uncle who ended up marrying Queen Mary and being accused of murdering her husband and King James's father, was agitated. A young man just shy of 30 years of age and in the prime of his life, but he didn't look like it taking one look at his face.

He had led a splendid life given his family relations within the inner echelons of the Scottish political class and was given a senior position as Commendator of Culcross Abbey. At the time he was only a baby, receiving the position when Lord Maitland stepped away. The Earl studied at St Andrews University in Scotland before following the typical route of getting educated on the continent, studying in France (where else) but also in Italy. He stayed there until recalled by King James to work in the country supporting him.

The Earl took to a role of power and influence very well although quickly betrayed King James in the Raid of Ruthven joining the side of the Lords who imprisoned him for over a year. It was King James's kindness, or some might say weakness, that meant the Earl had a second chance of redemption following that incident.

The Earl played a key part in the Treaty of Berwick, ensuring peace between England and Scotland. He really believed in Scottish nationalism and superiority over the English. It was therefore no surprise that when Queen Mary was executed, he led the faction that believed the correct response would be to invade England. Calmer heads prevailed, but the Earl had his moment of shining glory. He was Lord High Admiral of the Scottish Navy when the Spanish Armada were defeated. Whilst this might have been down to the weather and rocky shoreline rather than military guile, it was a proud moment in Scottish naval history and one that the Earl revelled in.

Unfortunately, the Earl's treasonous nature couldn't

be contained for too long and he was one of the key lords behind another plot to seize the King and Lord Maitland from Holyroodhouse, only being foiled when neither were there. He was therefore found guilty of treason a few months earlier, with the punishment still to be decided by the King.

His hurried manner was therefore clearly of someone who had escaped wherever they were being held and was here to seek Lord Sinclair's help. Heaven only knows what he would have done if he knew that the King and Lord Maitland were sleeping only a few feet away from the stairs he was racing up. He was in such a hurry he skipped and missed the steps as he flew up them.

Upon reaching the top of the landing, he couldn't quite remember which room was Lord Maitland's and which was Lady Maitland's. He definitely didn't want to make a mistake at this time of night. Little did he know that if he chose rightly, and chose Lord Maitland's usual bedchamber, then he would actually burst in and see King James fast asleep with the poets Mark and William.

He continued pondering and just didn't remember. He therefore rushed back downstairs to ask the Head of the Household, who was making his way up the stairs to confront the Earl.

"Which room is the Master's bedchamber?" asked the Earl.

"It's the one on the left, but.." said the Head of the Household, but before he could finish what he wanted to say the Earl had already flown back up the stairs and was now fast approaching the master's bedchamber.

He knocked forcefully on it but didn't wait for a response before opening it. It was dark with no candlelight visible, so the Earl went back into the landing to take the candle there and walked back into the room towards the King's bed.

"Lord Sinclair, Lord Sinclair, wake up. I need to speak with you," said the Earl.

The bed's occupants woke, and it began with Mark and William who both got up in unison.

That the bed had two participants startled the Earl, especially given that they were men. He couldn't quite make out who they were, but he was surprised as he never thought Lord Sinclair was that way inclined.

"What on earth are you doing here? I think three is enough, don't you?" asked William in an annoyed tone.

The King was passed out and still snoring.

"Lord Sinclair?" asked a hesitant Earl.

"This is the King's bed for tonight, now bog off!" instructed William.

The Earl was shell shocked and left the room, apologising profusely on his way out. He had escaped such a close shave. The man who had sentenced him to treason was only feet away. How lucky he was to have escaped with his life.

He then proceeded to the Lady's bedchamber, assuming that Lord Sinclair was therefore sleeping in the same bedchamber as his wife. He approached the door and knocked forcefully.

"Lord Sinclair, I need to speak with you," bellowed the Earl.

Before he opened the door, the door had swung open, and there was Lord Maitland stood there.

"The Earl of Bothwell, what a pleasure it is to see you. I thought you were enjoying the Majesty's facilities in detention?" Said Lord Maitland.

Before he gave the stunned Earl a chance to respond, he immediately called out for guards to come at the top of his voice.

"Guards, Guards, seize this man! The Earl is a wanted man," bellowed Lord Maitland.

The entire castle was awake with all the commotion, and everybody on all floors had left their rooms to see what was going on.

The Earl quickly realised that this was no place for him, and much like Claude earlier on, he scarpered back down the stairs like a rocket and was heading to the door. Before he reached the door, Lord Maitland screamed, "You can run Bothwell, but that is all you can do. You can never be at peace!"

And with that, the Earl of Bothwell was gone. He jumped on his horse and cantered off at quite some speed into the night.

The King had awoken by now and made his way to the landing and asked, "who was that?"

"That, your Majesty, was the Earl of Bothwell," replied Lord Maitland.

"The Earl of Bothwell. How dare he. He has caused my family enough problems over the years. Him and all the Bothwell clan are no good, but they garner significant support."

"I know, we need to figure out a way to nullify him. Don't worry, I'll fix it," said Lord Maitland.

"Good good, but don't forget to involve Lord Sinclair, he has a wise head for matters like these," replied the King.

Lord Maitland was a little upset that he wasn't trusted to solve a matter like this, but he accepted why the King asked for Lord Sinclair's involvement.

Lord Sinclair too had awoken and was on the landing.

"I'm sorry gentlemen, I hear that the commotion was the Earl of Bothwell who had come to see me," said Lord Sinclair.

"Why would he see you?" asked Lord Maitland.

"Yes, why?" said the King joining in.

All eyes were now pointing at Lord Sinclair, and he didn't like where this conversation was headed.

"Gentlemen, let's keep our heads. My Head of Household informed me that he was actually here to see me. I do not understand why. He perhaps wanted some advice or to beg for forgiveness," said Lord Sinclair.

"Perhaps - but if he wanted to beg for forgiveness then now would have been an opportune moment, don't you agree?" replied Lord Maitland.

"I do, but I think we startled the poor chap," said Lord Sinclair. "First, he enters my bedchamber finding the King and then he enters Lady Sinclair's bedchamber and finds Lord Maitland. That would be enough of a surprise to send even the most regretful of men scampering out of the castle and riding for the hills."

This made logical sense, which the King and Lord Maitland accepted. After all of this commotion it would be difficult to go back to sleep, so the Lords went for a smoke of tobacco to relax the senses. This couldn't have been done in the open, so they feigned yawning and waited for the King to head back to his bedchamber before going for a smoke.

They leaned against one window to have a look at the night sky with their pipes now lit and a dim of smoke being built up.

"What a night," said Lord Maitland.

"Yes, a memorable one for sure," said Lord Sinclair. "I'm not sure what to make of it. We had The Ambassador make his way here all the way from London. Entertainment from some of Scotland's finest poets. The Moore. Who can forget about him? A feast that took a month of planning. We had the King and his *personal* entertainment. Claude returned, finally. The auction was a massive success. The game of noddy. And the Earl of Bothwell's late interlude."

"I must admit, you laid on a magnificent event and I'm sure the King will be thankful in the morning," admitted Lord Maitland grudgingly.

"Thank-you. Coming from you, that is a compliment," replied Lord Sinclair.

And with that, they stubbed out their tobacco, patted each other on the back and headed upstairs back to sleep. There had been enough excitement for one banquet.

CHAPTER ELEVEN

The Morning After

L ord Sinclair was the first to wake, or so he assumed. At the first glimmer of daylight through the windows, the Lord was up and already downstairs to ensure that breakfast preparations were underway. It was downstairs that he discovered that the poets had already departed - an engagement in Edinburgh was what the servants told him.

The weather did not look good. Storm clouds were on the horizon and even though it was daylight, it was quite dark, which made it appear to be early evening on a summer's day rather than the morning.

It was quite a sight in the kitchen with servants and chefs scurrying around. The whiff of freshly baked bread in the morning was delightfully enjoyed by Lord Sinclair. It would be bread, sage, and butter for breakfast served with a nice ale to wash away any hangovers from the previous evening's festivities.

The Melville's were next to wake. Jane had barely slept a wink, still tormented by the curse placed upon her. Andrew had spent the night reassuring her that they would take legal action to find out whether the woman was a witch or a fraud but Jane didn't want to bring any attention to their predicament and thought it was best to just forget it, although that was easier said than done.

"Lord Sinclair, it really smells nice down here," said Andrew.

"Why, thank-you," responded Lord Sinclair. "After all that trouble last night, I'm hoping that the smell of fresh bread will act as a kind of aromatherapy for calming nerves."

"Well, I think you might need to do the opposite of a rain dance because I don't think that storm that is headed this way will calm anyone," observed Andrew.

Lord Sinclair scrunched his face but didn't want to face reality for the time being, still hoping that the storm might be diverted elsewhere.

Nobody would begin breakfast until the King was up, so Lord Sinclair and the Melville's continued their discussion in the kitchen. It was Lord Sinclair's home and the Melville's were used to being around in kitchens so they thought nothing of the informality. It was reassuringly cosy.

There was however an awkward silence as they really didn't know what to say to each other, Andrew broke the silence, "So I hear that the University of Copenhagen have built a dormitory."

"A dormitory?" asked a puzzled Lord Sinclair.

"Yes, Valkendorfs Kollegium is what it's called. It's where the students can sleep and live whilst they are studying. It used to be a monastery before a chap called Valkendorfs bought it and turned it into a dormitory."

"Whatever will the Danish think of next. I guess with Anne - we'll have more of these Scandinavian ideas permeating here," replied Lord Sinclair.

The silence had returned. Although, it was now even more awkward than before given that the attempt to kick start some natural conversation had failed.

It was now Lord Sinclair's turn, "I heard that Job of Moscow had been announced as the first ever Patriarch of Moscow and all of Russia."

Andrew was ashamed as he didn't know what a Patriarch was. Jane saw this and stepped in, it was less embarrassing if she interrupted, "Sorry Lord Sinclair, what is a Patriarch and who is this Job?"

"Ahh Jane, now that is a question! Andrew - why can't you ask intelligent questions like this?" remarked Lord Sinclair. Andrew was sure that Lord Sinclair was trying to wind him up, but Lord Sinclair continued, "The Patriarch is the Bishop of Moscow and also head of the Russian Orthodox Church. It was a gigantic step for them to announce their first ever head. Similar to the power struggles we had here between Religion and Kings. In Russia, they have Tsars who rule and this upset many people so some of that power was transferred to the Patriarchs so effectively you now will have a political battle between Tsars and Patriarchs as to who runs the country. That they have even appointed a Patriarch means that Tsar Fyodor is weak."

Jane feigned interest but as soon as she heard that it was about more political infighting she switched off, she had seen enough of that in Scotland and England so had little interest in learning more about the problems in

Russia.

The awkward silence had once again returned. Luckily, Lady Sinclair was the next to awaken and headed downstairs to join her husband.

"I see you are all here in the kitchen, I too love the smell of bread in the morning. Isn't it calming?" remarked Lady Sinclair.

Before anyone could respond, thunder was heard in the distance and then lightning could be seen. It looked as if the storm was headed closer. Lord Sinclair sighed and had now accepted his fate that the storm was indeed headed to Knockhall.

"Secure the horses, border up the windows and doors. Let's batten down the hatches," was the order from Lord Sinclair to his Head of the Household.

Servants then scurried around to make it happen. A few minutes later they returned having complied but hadn't ordered up the King's or Lord Maitland's rooms.

"What shall we do?" asked the Head of the Household.

"Leave the King to sleep. Have someone ready to border it up as soon as he wakes. As for Lord & Lady Maitland, wake them up - their security is of the paramount importance," said Lord Sinclair with a wry smile. It might be a minor victory, but he would savour any way of getting one back at Maitland.

A few minutes later, Lord and Lady Maitland headed downstairs towards the kitchen. Upon arriving, Lord Maitland was in a foul mood, displeased at the early rude awakening." What is this? A peasant's convention. Can we all gather like civilised people and await the King's arrival in the banqueting hall? This isn't Ulster, you know," said Lord Maitland in a condescending tone.

Lord Sinclair blushed slightly as he knew that Lord Maitland was right. The kitchen was no place for the Lord and definitely no place for the Lord and five others. So, they all made their way to the banqueting hall, still awaiting the King. Whilst it was no longer possible to see outside given that the windows were bordered up - the wind could be heard howling, testing the barricades outside. The thunder was now closer and the lightning more frequent. The storm was here.

Jane was nervous and clung tightly to Andrew. Elsewhere in the castle, a servant could be heard shouting that the King had awoken. This was unsurprising, given that there was now a violent storm underway.

The King entered the banqueting hall.

"Good Morning, your Majesty," said Lord Sinclair invitingly.

"Morning, Sinclair," replied the King, slightly flustered. "Where are the poets? I don't see them anywhere."

"Unfortunately, they left at the crack of dawn as they had other commitments."

The King muttered something incomprehensible and then sat down. A lightning bolt struck nearby, which threw the King off balance. Lord Maitland stifled a snigger.

"I see we are in for a rough day," said the King.

Breakfast was brought out by the servants. The whiff of fresh bread was now a fixture of the banqueting hall. It lifted the mood in the room immediately.

The King sat on his chair, looked around the room and saw Lord Sinclair sat next to Lady Sinclair - they were at peace next to each other. Lord Maitland sat next to Lady Maitland - they looked distant from one another. The Melville's were there together - cosy as always.

The King then blurted out, "Where is the Ambassador?"

This panicked the rest of the room, which were left wondering why they had forgotten about him. He was an elderly man, and the storm was violently loud now. Could he have passed away in his sleep?

Upon seeing a lack of leadership in the room, the King instructed everyone to follow him, so they all did as they were told. One-by-one in single file up the staircase to the top and into the Ambassador's room. There was an air of trepidation as they stepped into the room, concerned what they may find. The King sent Lord Sinclair first in. Lord Sinclair creaked open the door to be greeted by a motionless Ambassador lying on his bed. He didn't appear to be breathing. Lord Sinclair wasn't keen on moving closer until prodded to by the King. He crept closer and was now right next to the bed. The Ambassador didn't appear to be breathing. He didn't know what to do, so shrugged his shoulders.

"Have a listen to his mouth to see if he is breathing," encouraged the King.

Lord Sinclair therefore leaned down to the Ambassadors mouth to have a listen. The Ambassador farted and coughed out some flem into Lord Sinclair's ear. The Ambassador awoke, surprised by the intrusion. Lord Sinclair was startled and disgusted at the same time whilst the King was laughing hysterically. The Ambassador was okay.

And with the excitement over, everyone except the Ambassador returned to the banqueting hall to finish breakfast.

The wind was now really howling outside. It didn't look like anybody would leave soon. The King gestured for Lord Sinclair to come over to him.

"Yes, your Majesty," said Lord Sinclair.

"You remember that young indigenous woman that you brought to my chamber last night? Have her in my chamber in five minutes. If I am stuck here, then I might as well enjoy myself," said the King laughing to himself.

"I'm afraid that she left last night. All the performers left immediately for another show many miles away," said Lord Sinclair with a slightly trembling voice.

The King again muttered something incomprehensible and waved away Lord Sinclair, who didn't need a second invitation and scarpered. The look on the King was now one of annoyance as to why the Gods had subjected him to this.

There wasn't much conversation in the room. The food had been cleared away and without the poets the energy and noise in the room was much lower than it had been the previous evening.

Lord Sinclair asked Lord Maitland to discuss a serious matter with him elsewhere. Lord Maitland didn't need to know more. He was pleased to leave the room. They made their way up the stairs to what was Lord Maitland's chambers the previous evening. Lord Sinclair closed the door carefully behind him and took out some tobacco from his jacket. Lord Maitland laughed and remarked, "you sneaky fellow."

"Well, the King has got me stressed. I can see that every minute that this storm continues will lead to a more difficult King."

"Don't fret, fellow. It will all be over soon," said Lord Maitland reassuringly.

"But what if it isn't?" asked Lord Sinclair.

"In that case, you'll be doomed," replied Lord Maitland giving off a snigger.

They both then enjoyed the tobacco and had a moment of serene quiet. Smoke being blown by the two gentlemen with Lord Maitland blowing smoke rings. Their moment enjoying the calm and peace came to a crashing end when the door swung open and there was the King. They were caught red handed smoking. The King was bored, so had ventured upstairs to join the men. The look on his face was one of disappointment, but he was resigned to his fate so didn't kick up a fuss. The King once again just muttered something incomprehensible and left, closing the door behind him.

"Do you think we are in trouble?" asked Lord Sinclair.

"Most definitely, but don't worry us naughty schoolboys will take our beatings like a man," replied Lord Maitland strongly slapping Lord Sinclair on the back with his booming laugh once again reaching out.

When they had finished smoking, they both returned to the banqueting hall, which really was a sorry sight. The King sat on his chair, looking bored. Lady Maitland

and Lady Sinclair were sat next to each other but not really saying anything. The Ambassador who had made his way to join everyone looked as if he was counting the seconds until this was all over. What a contrast this sight was from just the evening before when it was a banquet, the likes of which people would remember for ages.

Lord Sinclair couldn't dwell too much on his own self pity as there was a sudden crash from above. Everyone jumped up, curious as to what it was. The King bellowed out, "Come, let's go to the dovecot, I assume."

Everyone did as they were told, so they all followed the King up the stairs to the dovecot. And there was Claude making lots of commotion, much like during the previous evening. Everyone still had the memory of yesterday in the front of their minds and were worried about the fate that was about to bestow Claude. The King didn't have his normal glimmer in his eye. He seemed resigned to being stuck in this awful place with no beloved poets, or even the indigenous woman to keep him company, so the King just muttered something incomprehensible and went back downstairs. Everyone was pleased that this was the result but a little concerned as they hadn't seen the King behave like this too often, so they were fearful for what would happen next.

The hours had passed, and we were now into the late afternoon with no let up in the weather. The Ambassador seizing the opportunity approaching the King.

"I am wondering if I could have a few moments of your time to discuss a private matter?"

"I guess that would be ok, what else am I to do," asked the King to himself.

They made their way up the stairs to the King's quarters and sat down, ready to talk.

"Your Majesty, many think of me as an old fool, but the New World is the future. Mark my words, in times to come it will be an empire and frontier that will pave unlimited riches for he who is brave enough to conquer it."

The King groaned. The Ambassador must have had the curse of the old with his memory failing him.

"Whilst the recent expeditions by the English have been unsuccessful,", continued the Ambassador. "There is untapped potential. Previous issues have been the strategy taken. Guns or butter has been the problem. Previous expeditions have either been too heavily focused on either the military side or the trading side. The solution requires balance. That way the indigenous people will respect and fear your armies but, will welcome them for all that they can bring."

The King groaned at having the same conversation as the previous evening. He figured that the Ambassador won't remember this conversation, so he just agreed to fund the expedition and then muttered something incomprehensible before leaving to return downstairs. The Ambassador was left sitting with a beaming smile across his face before eventually following the King back downstairs.

Everyone was hungry, so the King instructed Lord Sinclair to bring out the food. Lord Sinclair complied and asked the servants to serve the food. A few minutes passed and what came out was Ox Soup and more bread. No ale or wine.

"What is this?" asked the King.

"I'm sorry your Majesty," said a trembling Lord Sinclair, "we were cleaned out yesterday of all the food and alcohol so this is all we have left."

"Ok, before we eat let the poets bless our food and peak our spirits," instructed the King.

"I'm afraid the poets left this morning, remember?" replied Lord Sinclair.

The King once again just muttered something incomprehensible and waved that everybody could eat. The meal was taken in silence with no conversation. What a sorry sight compared to the extravagance that was on display the previous evening.

The meal was finished and everyone just went straight to bed. This storm was keeping them together for another night, at least. Who knew how long this storm would continue for? It isn't inconceivable that it might last for days, or even a week, that had happened before in the brutal Scottish climate.

CHAPTER TWELVE

In the middle of the night, Lord Sinclair was woken by some commotion. He went downstairs and could hear the roar of horses in the distance. Still half asleep, he couldn't quite get his bearings. He could hear that the storm seemed to have abated. He therefore opened the door and just got a glimpse of the King's procession departing. It looked like the King took the first opportunity of the let up in the storm to leave. This wasn't wholly unusual, as the King attending your home was a big enough privilege. Lord Sinclair went back inside, relieved that the King had departed and slept soundly until the morning.

In the morning, the storm had been replaced with a bright sunny day. After breakfast, it was time for the guests to depart. Lord & Lady Maitland were the next to depart.

"Sinclair, I was worried I would be trapped in your company for days given how the storm was raging but I'm glad it was only two nights. I guess that you put on a decent banquet," said Lord Maitland.

"Thank-you Lord Maitland. Selfless as always in your ability to give compliments," replied Lord Sinclair. The two friends/enemies shook hands and Lord & Lady Maitland departed in their carriage, and off they went back to their life of wealth and privilege.

Next to leave were the Melvilles.

"Thank-you so much for inviting us, we will remember tonight forever and really appreciate us being part of the celebrations," said Andrew.

"Yes, I really enjoyed it. It helped take my mind off things a little but I'm really grateful to have been here," contributed Jane.

"That's ok. In fact, the King asked me to request that you, Jane, go to greet and collect Anne of Denmark when she arrives in Scotland," said Lord Sinclair.

"Wow, I would be honoured," replied Jane.

"See," said Andrew, "your luck is turning already. This is the start of a bright future. You might end up being best friends!"

They were a bit too grateful, showing their awkwardness and appreciation more than a more refined guest would have, but Lord Sinclair didn't mind this. He quite liked the fact that they were so happy to have been a guest of his.

"It was a pleasure to have you here, have a safe journey back," wished Lord Sinclair as the Melvilles departed.

Finally, it was the Ambassador's turn. He was dressed impeccably like all elderly gentleman of that day. He looked tired, and Lord Sinclair was concerned whether he could survive the lengthy journey back.

"Don't worry," said the Ambassador. "We'll stop along the way in York for two days to rest and take care of some business. I'll then finish the journey back to London."

And with that - the last guest had departed. It was now just Lord, and Lady Sinclair stood in the doorway of their magnificent castle. They had pulled it off. They had hosted a banquet fit for a King. And with that, they went back inside to unwind after the stresses of the last 48 hours.

III

The Aftermath

CHAPTER THIRTEEN

King James's Legacy

Political

The banquet was politically charged. Whether it was discussions on English battles or King James's own traumatic past - all roads led to political turmoil.

It is therefore no surprise that King James left a political legacy and changed the landscape of England, Scotland, Europe, and the United States for many years to come.

First King of England and Scotland.

King James VI did eventually become the first king of a united England and Scotland. He was known as King James VI of Scotland and King James I of England. This happened in March 1603. Shortly after his accession to the English throne, the King left Edinburgh for London and promised to return every three years, much like he did in his conversation with Lord Maitland.

However, his head was turned by London and he rarely ended up visiting Scotland, both breaking his promise and his principles whereby a King should remain in touch with his subjects. He was in awe of the wealth of England, both as a country and what the people had. He was quoted as saying, "I've swapped a stony couch for a deep feather bed."

King James liked the Tower of London as Lord Maitland predicted. The menagerie of wild animals was a treat for all of London to enjoy, not just the King. Under his reign the collection was extended to include three eagles, two pumas, a tiger, a jackal, and more lions and leopards. He also had the lions' den refurbished so that visitors could see more of the lions prowling around. He also wanted the experience to be enhanced so visitors could also see the lions drink and wash themselves.

King James's cruelty towards Lord Sinclair's homing pigeon Claude was nothing compared to the popular sport of bear baiting that thrived during King James's reign. In this sport, a bear would be chained to a stake by its leg or neck and then vicious dogs would be unleashed in the bear pit to attack the bear to see who would survive. The bear would always be saved before death, as the cost of bringing bears from abroad was significant. Two streets in London called *Bear Gardens* and *Bear Lane* still exist today as a gruesome reminder of what used to take place on those spots many years ago.

However, things were far from ideal. England was heavily in debt, a legacy of the wars that Elizabeth had fought. King James's priority was to establish a single country under one King, one parliament and one law. In 1604, the English Parliament refused his title to become King of Great Britain on legal grounds. This didn't stop the King, who used the title anyway and forced the Scottish Parliament to acknowledge it.

There were several plots against the King. The closest to succeeding was by Guido Fawkes, the angry young Catholic man that the Ambassador met in York on his journey to the banquet. He was more commonly known as Guy Fawkes and on the eve of the 5th of November 1605 was camped under the English Parliament with 36 barrels of gunpowder that he hoped to blow up the Houses of Parliament killing the King in the process. The plot failed, and it is still an annual tradition today in England to celebrate the failure with firework displays.

The King frequently had run-ins with Parliament and prorogued it when he became fed up by their resistance to his ideas. At its worse, Parliament was closed for years at a time and the King ruled like a dictator.

After the gunpowder plot, the King sought to control English Catholics to a greater extent. Various laws were passed forcing allegiance to be sworn to the King over the Pope. To avoid the confusion of different translations and discrepancies amongst the approved books of the Bible, King James commissioned an official version to be put together. The Authorised King James Bible as it is known was completed in 1611 and is still in widespread use today.

The King's stubborn belief in the divine right of Kings and his period of self rule coupled with financial irresponsibility led the foundations for the English Civil War. The seeds of that stubbornness and financial irresponsibility was nothing new as he had the same traits whilst King of Scotland. What really made things much worse was that after becoming King of England, the sheer wealth of England enabled his delusions of grandeur to go even further.

King James passed away in 1625. His son Charles I took the brunt of that anger in 1649 when he was the first (and only) King of England to be executed by the people which led to Great Britain becoming a Republic for 11 years until the monarchy was re-established and continues to this day.

The English Armada.

The English Armada in 1589 which had been such a colossal failure financially and politically was a key gripe of the guests attending the banquet. The consequence of that failure led to a combined Anglo-Dutch force putting pressure on the Spanish which had conquered large parts of Dutch land. Successful victories in Breda in 1591 kick started new confidence amongst the English forces, and many Dutch cities fell back into Dutch control. The English were well compensated for their contribution in freeing the Dutch from complete Spanish rule.

However, the Spanish were far from beaten and were re-equipping their ships ready for more bloody battles. What turned the war in England's favour was the introduction of the private sector into the war. Several self funded war ships attacked Spanish assets with the blessing of Queen Elizabeth - their reward for any victories over the Spanish was the right to keep any treasures they found. By the end of the war, nearly 1,000 vessels had been seized by this private army. However, this merely maintained the status quo as the Spanish were too powerful to be fully defeated.

By the end of the 16th Century, the war had been costly for all sides and they had all become battle weary.

Spain had a new King and was desperate to make peace. However, their demands were to maintain the current land that they owned across the continent. Something that wasn't acceptable to England or the Dutch. It was only after King James made his eventual ascent to the throne of England in 1603 that peace did finally come through the Treaty of London in 1604. The new Kings of England and Spain saw the pain that the war had inflicted on both sides, and it was only when the previous rulers had passed away that peace could be made.

The key terms agreed were that Spain would accept that England would not be Catholic and would stop further direct or indirect attempts to influence it in that direction. In return, England allowed Spanish merchant ships to pass through English waters and removed all military and financial support for the Dutch rebels. This treaty did not go down well in England with many feeling they were abandoning the Dutch. The Spanish were delighted seeing a chance to seize control.

The Dutch fended off Spain until 1609, partially due to unofficial support from England. Eventually, Spain had become bankrupt from the costly wars, so a truce was signed between Spain and the Dutch which established the Dutch Republic.

King James further built ties with Spain by arranging the marriage of his son, the Prince of Wales to Maria Anna, the King of Spain's daughter. This caused uproar in Parliament because of the King's family marrying into the Catholic Spanish Royal household. The marriage didn't go ahead as there was too much political pressure and also because the Prince of Wales and Maria wouldn't convert to the other's religion.

The New World.

The two previous attempts to settle in the New World in the 1580s had been massive failures, so the Ambassador's attempts to try again were scoffed at. The mystery surrounding the *Lost Colony* was never solved. Some theories suggest that the colonists assimilated with the Native Americans and that some of those in the villages had European features. Others believe that they tried to rescue themselves by attempting to sail back to England, but that the ship sank during the journey. Finally, they could have been slaughtered by the Native Americans or attacked by the Spanish. Despite immense interest, there has not been any archaeological evidence discovered to solve the mystery.

The timing of the Ambassador's plans had been poor given the negative impact of the English Armada on the confidence in British naval power. However, this made sense for an ambitious King James who kept the idea in the back of his mind. After taking the English throne, a joint stock company was setup in 1606, the Virginia Company, in a similar structure to the company that was setup to facilitate trade with Russia by the Ambassador all those years earlier.

The Virginia Company led two voyages to the New World within a year. One voyage had 105 men and 39 sailors who travelled for 144 days before they finally arrived in the New World. To avoid attack, they sailed westward until they reached a shoreline they felt was defendable and established Jamestown, named after King James. Investors received gold and other minerals sent back to England, but the success of the colony depended on regular trading.

The only problem with the location was that it was largely cut off from the mainland and had little hunting or fresh drinking water and limited farmland.

The second voyage had about 100 men who sailed for three months and eventually landed at Maine, but because of limited resources, it failed and they sailed back to England within a year.

It was therefore feared that the first voyage would also be a failure because of a lack of resources. Supply ships were instructed to head to the New World to support the colonisation. In 1612, several supply ships found themselves in hurricane-force winds and ended up stranded in Bermuda. The Virginia Company therefore claimed the land as their own and spun off a separate company called the Somers Isles Company that controlled Bermuda until 1684, which is when the King of England took control of it. Something that continues to this day.

Some supply ships continued on to Jamestown and were shocked by what they found. Starvation was rife with 80% of settlers dying, and there was evidence of cannibalism by the survivors. The supply ships that returned to England told of the hardships and the need to abandon the colony. However, a certain Lord Delaware refused to accept this. The new supply ships would be well stocked with food, doctors and more colonists. Lord Delaware was also a war monger - he didn't look for peace with the locals. He sought to capture the land that they needed to survive and after several successful raids - Jamestown had become a permanent colony.

The Native Americans didn't give up. The wars continued in the 1620s and the 1630s. In 1633, a truce was agreed with the Native Americans. To celebrate the end of hostilities, a toast of liquor was had by over 200 Native Americans and the colonists. Only problem was that the colonists had poisoned the liquor and the Native Americans died or were too weak to avoid slaughter. It wasn't until 1646 that peace was finally agreed with the tribes pleading allegiance to the King of England and in return received some land that the colonists deemed unimportant.

Jamestown was an enormous success driven by tobacco exports that made it a thriving and important asset for the King. In 1624, King James revoked the Virginia Company's charter and took control of the colony himself meaning that Virginia would be a Commonwealth of England until 1775 run by a Colonial Governor. It was the English that changed the capital of Virginia to Williamsburg in 1699, and eventually when the United States declared independence from England in 1775, Virginia became one of the original 13 states. Without King James's ambition and determination to succeed then the history of the United States would have been very different.

Ulster and Northern Ireland.

One of the Ambassador's other ideas was to start a plantation in Ulster. Something that Lord Sinclair agreed with. Ulster wasn't civilised and was very rural. King James again waited until he was King of England to begin, and it wasn't until 1606 that wealthy landowners started private plantations. The aim was to control, anglicise, and instil civilisation in Ulster. It was the region that had been the most resistant to English rule, so had to be controlled.

This meant that English judges were now in charge and

didn't recognise any Irish titles to the land. It was also a British venture (joint English and Scottish), one of the first instances of Britain showing its might in the world. Most of the settlers were Scottish as King James was mindful that now he was living in London he didn't want the Scots to think he was only focused on the English so as a reward he proclaimed that most of the land would go to his loyal Scots.

To ensure that the plantation was a success, as previous attempts had failed, the plan was to confiscate all the land and then re-distribute it. A quarter of the land would remain for the Irish, but on the proviso they used English or Scottish workers.

As appears to be the way with these ventures, private investors funded the project.

The plantation had mixed success. The excitement of the Virginia Company trumped the Ulster plantation, so the private investment all went towards the New World. By the 1630s, the plantation had 80,000 Brits, probably less than half the total population.

The plan to convert the population to Protestant values also struggled because of language barriers. From the 1640s onwards, the battles became more violent with the Ulster Catholics staging rebellions. Northern Ireland was formed in 1921 to formalise the land owned by the Protestant and Catholic populations, but the desire for a unified Ireland remains. King James's legacy by bringing Protestants to Ulster continues to create problems centuries after that decision was taken.

Interestingly, in 1611 King James granted William Fowler 2,000 acres (8 Sq Km) of land in Ulster as a reward for his service to the King. We can only speculate why the King granted such vast amounts of land to William. Most of the land he received was in an area called Moyglass, and the islands of Inishfomer, Galleran, and Lougherne. He sold it all in 1615 to Sir John Hume.

CHAPTER FOURTEEN

King James's Legacy

Lovers

K ing James had an eventful night at the banquet, having close relations with both men and women. He was subject to rumour throughout his reign, and in history there has been significant research and discussion as to the extent of his personal relationships. The gossip surrounding his relationship with Esme Stewart was rife in 1589 and it is widely acknowledged today that Esme played a key part in the King's life.

The King's never forgot about him despite their relatively brief time together. After his death, he looked after all of his family and instructed his son and successor Charles I to do the same. As a result, Esme's family had considerable influence in both the Scottish and English Courts over the next two generations.

The King's next enormous love was Anne of Denmark. He was infatuated with her at the start and they had a strong and loving marriage until around 1606, which is when they were living apart. It affected both of them deeply. King James had lost interest in his wife and Anne as a result had become sad and reclusive, rarely making public appearances. When she passed away, the King was genuinely heartbroken and composed a poem in her memory. It took him a long time to get over her passing.

Despite his love for her, he was not fateful almost from the start of their marriage, having an affair between 1593 and 1595 with Anne Murray, who later became Lady Glamis. He wrote poems about her, calling her, "my mistress and my love."

The King and Anne had eight children, but during that time it was rare for babies to survive to adult age. They were lucky and had three grow up: Henry, Prince of Wales; Elizabeth and Charles I. Unfortunately, Henry died from typhoid fever at 18, so Charles was his natural heir.

While the King seemed to enjoy both the company of women and men during his early years, the latter years had rumours of very strong relationships with men.

The first was with Robert Carr in 1607. Carr was only 17 years old whilst King James was 51 years old. He was a strong young handsome man taking part in a jousting contest that the King was in attendance at. A simple young man, not very bright, but he had muscles the size of pheasants. During the contest, Carr was knocked from his horse and broke his leg. The King took a shine to Carr looking after him, and they stayed in touch. He was made Gentleman of the Bedchamber, the role that required guarding of the bedchamber and keeping the King company at night.

As King James had done previously, he bestowed title after title on Carr. Carr became Knight of the Garter, a Privy Counsellor, and Viscount Rochester. Their personal relationship ran into difficulties because Carr eventually fell in love with another woman who he was desperate to marry. However, he needed the King's help to gain her a divorce from her husband. The King helped, and as a wedding present granted Carr the title of the Earl of Somerset.

That was not the end of the matter. In 1615, a letter was written by the King displeased that Carr had withdrawn from lying in his bed chamber although they had been together hundreds of times. This created a public scandal, and when it was revealed that Carr's wife had poisoned an opponent of the marriage, the King took his revenge and forcefully insisted that they stand trial. Carr threatened to reveal everything about his sexual relationship with the King if he was to go to prison. The King was so scared of this that two men were posted besides Carr during his trial, with instructions to muffle him if he did so. He didn't. He refused to admit guilt, but his wife did. They were both sentenced to death, but the King lessened the sentence instead imprisoning them in the Tower of London for seven years after which they could retire to the countryside.

The King's other big relationship was with George Villiers. He was the son of a Leicestershire knight and they met in 1614. Villiers was incredibly handsome with piercing blue eyes, a strong jawline, and thick black hair. He was intelligent and honest. A step up from Carr.

As the King liked to do, he bestowed title after title on Villiers as well: Knight of the Garter; Viscount Villiers;

Earl of Buckingham; and the Marquess of Buckingham.

What was unusual here was that after being together for eight years, Villiers was then the first commoner in over 100 years to be made a Duke, receiving the title of Duke of Buckingham.

The King wasn't shy of his love for Villiers, comparing his love to that of Jesus's love of John. Villiers became an excellent friend of Anne of Denmark. Villiers had become the unofficial husband to the King. King James even referred to him as such. They primarily stayed in Apethorpe Hall, which was the King's favourite Royal Residence, and whilst renovating it in 2008, a secret passage linking the bedchamber of King James and Villiers was found. Villiers was at the King's bedside when he passed away.

CHAPTER FIFTEEN

King James's Legacy

Marriage

King James knew that to preserve the Royal bloodline, he had to marry someone suitable and Anne of Denmark was the best match around. On the 20th of August 1589, that finally happened, a month after the banquet. At the Kronborg Castle in Denmark, the ceremony took place with the 5th Earl of Marischal sat next to Anne on the bridal bed where she became King James's wife. It was a marriage by proxy, with the Earl taking the place of King James - who was safely back in Scotland. This wasn't unusual as ensuring the marriage took place avoided any embarrassment should the bride or groom change his or her mind, much like Dudley did to Queen Mary all those years earlier.

King James was keen for Anne to begin her life as Queen as soon as possible. She left Denmark within 10 days on her ship *Gideon,* but there were a series of misfortunes that took place.

First, a naval gun had backfired, killing two gunners - a sign of terrible luck. As would be typical after such a tragic accident, a gun salute took place the next day. However, this too had grave misfortune. The gun exploded, killing one gunner and injuring a further nine of the crew.

Second, the weather had turned for the worse. Storms that hadn't been seen in Northern Europe for decades slammed waves against the shore pushing against any ships trying to make a journey on the seas. Anne's ship encountered extreme difficulties and went missing for three days. To compound matters, two of the ships in the flotilla collided, killing two more sailors.

Third, if that wasn't bad enough. Anne's ship, Gideon, sprang a dangerous leak and had to divert to Norway for repairs before it could safely continue on its journey. But it leaked again, so returned to dock. A month had now passed, and it was October, so the crews were unwilling to try again given the series of misfortunes that took place and the harsh Scandinavian winters that were about to hit the region.

King James really loved Anne. He heard reports of these issues throughout the period and asked for national fasting and public prayers to ensure safe passage for Anne. Rescue parties were sent. Songs written by the King told of the Greek mythological tale of Hero & Leander to compare the current situation between King James and Anne. Leander was a young man who would swim every night across the sea to see Hero. Hero would light a lamp at the top of her tower to guide his way. Like all great tales, it had a tragic ending when one night Leander drowned on one of his visits to Hero. Upon hearing the news, Hero threw herself over the edge of the tower to her death to be with him.

Whilst this was going on, Andrew and Jane Melville

were also about to play their part. They spent a month after the banquet back at Rossend Castle, where they lived near Fife. Jane had been asked to greet Anne in Leith upon her arrival in Scotland and it was an incredible honour that would give her the opportunity to become one of the most important people in Anne's life providing her with immense power.

During the misfortune that was blighting Anne's progress to Scotland, Jane too had sea problems. The storms were powerful in Scotland as well. She was on a ferry boat crossing the river Forth between Burntisland and Leith when it capsized in the stormy weather with all but two of the passengers perishing to their death. Jane didn't survive. When Andrew found out, he was heartbroken. King James too was distraught, and his anxiety about Anne's arrival to Scotland multiplied. King James was angry - he was always wary of witches and knew that this level of grave misfortune was man made.

King James could not wait any longer and when he found out that Denmark had given up on the sailing, he immediately commissioned his own ship and took 300 advisors and servants with him to personally make the journey. He successfully arrived in Oslo on the 19th of November 1589 after travelling by land from Flekkefjord via Tonsberg. Upon seeing her, he immediately gave her a kiss in public. This shocked Anne as this wasn't normal custom, and not for a lady - and a Royal one at that. However, she blushed and found this charming.

King James and Anne ended up having a formal wedding in November, with all the pomp and ceremony that you could imagine. The ceremony took place in French so they could both understand it. Anne was beautiful, a stunning bride.

With the marriage finally taking place, a month's worth of celebrations happened, so Lord Maitland's offer of beer to commemorate the occasion came in handy. King James really loved Anne, and the couple visited Kronborg Castle in Denmark to meet the Danish Royal family.

Anne was crowned in May 1590 in Holyroodhouse, which was the first Protestant coronation in Scotland. It was a seven hour ceremony, after which King James finally had his Queen.

CHAPTER SIXTEEN

King James's Legacy

The Author

King James shared a lot of his views throughout the banquet, arguably to anybody who would listen. He was a deep thinker and had strong views on nearly every topic. It was therefore no surprise to discover that he published his thoughts to imprint them on the masses.

His first work was published five years earlier called *The Essayes of a Prentise in the Divine Art of Poesie*, its original purpose to set a standard for all poets to continue writing in the Scottish tradition. It was therefore no surprise that the likes of William and Mark looked up to him. What is interesting about this first work from the King was that given the topic, it was never translated into English for publication in England.

The banquet and time spent with the poets really inspired King James. Two years later he published his guide on creative exercises titled *His Majesties Poeticall Exercises at Vacant Houres*.

However, it was the next four works by the King that

are remembered in history. His most famous work is arguably *Daemonologie*. King James was always fearful of witches, but the trauma of Anne's arrival in Scotland and the drowning of Jane led to significant repercussions.

The admiral of the Danish fleet escorting Anne to King James blamed the Danish Finance Minister for not sufficiently equipping the royal ship. To save his bacon, he in turn blamed witchcraft and named Karen the Weaver as the culprit for sending little demons in empty barrows who climbed on board the ships and caused the storms. After being arrested, and tortured, Karen named Anna Koldings as the main Danish witch. She too was tortured and confessed all. There was a group of women who would meet at the house of Karen, and Anna was the Mother of the Devil. She became a celebrity in prison and was found guilty and was burnt at the stake in Kronborg. Twelve women were executed for their involvement in the death of Jane and the troubles that Anne had in her voyage. It was when King James heard this that he set up his own tribunal.

The North Berwick Witch trials were the result, and in 1590 it saw several people accused of witchcraft for all those unbelievable incidents relating to Anne and Jane. The trials ran for over two years and it implicated 70 people, including the Earl of Bothwell, the mysterious stranger who appeared in the night seeking Lord Sinclair's help.

There were many witches accused such as Dr John Fian, a schoolmaster who had made a deal with the devil to receive immense witching power. He confessed to being one of the head sorcerers but pleaded for forgiveness renouncing his deal with the devil and promising to live a good Christian life. He stayed strong despite the devil visiting him personally the same evening, according to his testimony. Luck was on his side as he escaped prison by stealing a key from a guard, but it didn't last long as he was recaptured and then tortured to gain his confession. The details of the torture methods used are too gruesome to explain. He ended up burnt at the stake.

There were victims too, such as the Earl of Angus who was said to be under the spell of a disease so strange that no doctor could find a cure or remedy.

It wasn't just Dr John Fian who was accused. There were many who not only were accused but confessed under torture. They admitted meeting the devil in church at night and promising to the devil that they would poison the King and other members of the Royal household and sink any Royal ships. The other major witch of the North Berwick Witch trials was Agnes Sampson, an elderly midwife. Who knows, maybe she was the one who visited Jane and placed a curse on her. She was accused and resisted at first. The importance of Agnes had made its way to the King, so she was tortured and examined in the Royal court. Her first confession was that she caused the storm that killed Jane by sinking a dead cat which had attached to it parts of a dead man, into the sea near Leith. That was the secret of her powers.

Agnes admitted trying to source the King's shirt or other personal items to repeat the trick when he began his voyage to collect Anne. Agnes said that the devil appeared and offered to help her children and that as a widow she had no choice but to accept. She went to North Berwick and collected bones to make potions. Agnes was also known to make wax images, a precursor to a voodoo doll. She was tried under 53 charges of witchcraft, eventually confessing after having her head shaved and being stripped naked, tortured, and kept without sleep for days. Even then, she didn't confess until the third interrogation. Agnes was also burnt at the stake in Holyroodhouse on the 28th of January 1591.

To this day, a bald Agnes after being stripped and tortured is said to roam Holyroodhouse.

King James *Daemonologie* included details of the North Berwick Witch trials and his fears of witchcraft, but it went much further. It also covered the methods that demons used to bother troubled men, covered werewolves and vampires, and was also political as it sought to inform the good Christian population that it was ok to persecute a witch under religious law. His book was written in a dialogue style to make it more accessible. The main plot being that Philomathes hears news of witchcraft in the kingdom, which he is fascinated by but couldn't find anyone knowledgeable on it until he bumps into a philosopher named Epistemon. It also covered: Astrology; The devil's contract with man; Differences between sorcery and witchcraft; and the illusions of Satan and the many forms he appears in.

Daemonologie had a significant cultural impact and led to the increased persecution of women as witches until the early 17th century.

It also really made a significant impact on William Shakespeare who took many of the concepts from the trials and the book as a basis for his masterpiece, Macbeth.

The conversation that the King had with Lord Sinclair

on the divine right of Kings titled *True Law of Free Monarchies* was written in 1598 by King James. Essentially it is the belief that the King has been pre-selected before his birth and that the population hand over the choice of that King to the Gods. As the King has been entrusted with this responsibility, he is therefore not responsible to any earthly being. Anyone who disagreed with King James therefore disagreed with God.

Whilst King James pioneered the idea in Northern Europe, it wasn't anything radical. There had been many cases of King's previously holding that belief, King James only articulated it better than most. Even in the Bible, The Prophet Samuel anoints Saul and then David as King of Israel. When Saul wanted revenge and to Kill David. David wouldn't raise his hand because Saul had been anointed by God.

The book is accompanied by another titled *Basilikon Doron*, published a year later. It was more of a manual for future Kings. It was originally written as a private letter for Prince Harry, who was next in line. However, when he was struck down with Typhoid Fever at 18, it was later handed to Charles, his other son. The book was published in its thousands in London. At the banquet, the King's discussion with Mark captured the key content of this book.

Finally, King James hated tobacco as he frequently mentioned at the banquet and everybody knew this. The King really was a visionary in this aspect, he wrote the first anti-tobacco publication and warned about passive smoking and the dangers to the lungs hundreds of years before scientists reached the same conclusion. He also introduced one of the world's first taxes on tobacco in

1604 levying a tax of £1 for 3 pounds (nearly 1.5kg) of tobacco, which meant that the average worker would need to work for an entire week just to pay the tax on a daily tobacco habit. The tax didn't really succeed as it impinged on the New World colonies and did nothing to stop demand. The King therefore in 1624 revoked the Virginia Company's charter and took control of the colony & all the tobacco himself. One quote from the book was:

"Have you not reason then to bee ashamed, and to forbeare this filthie noveltie, so basely grounded, so foolishly received and so grossely mistaken in the right use thereof? In your abuse thereof sinning against God, harming your selves both in persons and goods, and raking also thereby the markes and notes of vanitie upon you: by the custome thereof making your selves to be wondered at by all forraine civil Nations, and by all strangers that come among you, to be scorned and contemned. A custome lothsome to the eye, hatefull to the Nose, harmefull to the braine, dangerous to the Lungs, and in the blacke stinking fume thereof, neerest resembling the horrible Stigian smoke of the pit that is bottomelesse."

- King James[1]

The most famous book that King James is associated with is the Bible. He commissioned an alternative version of it in 1603. The most commonly used Bible at the time was the Geneva Bible, which was the first mechanically produced widely available Bible. The problem with it was that King James didn't like the translation, which he thought was sloppy. He didn't like the style of it - too many annotations that distracted the reader, and too many references to the monarchy as tyrants. He therefore commissioned a new Bible. The Protestants preferred the Geneva version and King James's Bible sold poorly when launched in 1611. It was only when he banned printing of extra copies of the Geneva Version that his version gained in popularity. However, it didn't stop the Protestants. They continued to print copies of the Geneva version but dated them 1599 to get around the rule and that was the copy they took as they migrated to what would become the United States.

The King James Bible took off because it was mass produced cheaply and had a poetic language to it making it easy on the ear. Unsurprising given the King's love of the arts. Today over half of the Bibles in the world are the King James version.

CHAPTER SEVENTEEN

King James's Legacy

The Extravagances

K ing James was famous for spending more than he had. His household frequently went on strike, as shown at the banquet. The King overspent whilst on the throne in Scotland and despite also ascending to the wealthier English throne; he did the same there. He viewed the English crown as the promised land after years in the wilderness. The English Royal finances were in good health under Queen Elizabeth, as she was never married and didn't have any children.

However, King James was different with his children, wife, and male admirers to look after frequently paying off their debts for them. Prince Harry had £25,000 a year put aside for expenditure only for him, which is the average wage in the UK in the 2010s. The King spent £36,000 a year on royal clothing alone. This caused problems with the Parliament, who were not impressed at his lavish spending. He promised the days of heavy spending were over in 1610 and apologised for his extravagance blaming his previous humble surroundings in Scotland. Whilst he curbed his spending slightly, it really didn't change that much.

The King's favourite pastime was holding masques - the theatrical form of entertainment that took place at the banquet. The masque described at the banquet closely resembled what happened a few years later at Prince Harry's baptism.

A famous account of a masque in 1606 by Sir John Harrington described how the entertainers moved forwards whilst the Royal Court members fell backwards. A nod to the heavy drinking of the Court and of King James in particular. Masques had a story, such as the Queen of Sheba, as described by Sir John. The purpose of which was to bring the King gifts with the Spirits of Hope, Faith, Victory, Charity, and Peace all visiting the King.

However, it didn't go smoothly. The actress playing Queen Sheba tripped over the steps of the throne and sent her gifts flying. The actresses playing Hope and Faith were too drunk to speak a word, while Peace was annoyed that she couldn't make her way to the throne so struck anyone in her path with olive branches.

King James's enjoyment of masques led to the building of a Banqueting House. There was a temporary structure in place but the King wanted a permanent home so commissioned the famous Architect Robert Stickells to design one. The result was an ornate building, but it had a forest of columns that blocked much of the audience's view so when it burnt down because of a fire in 1619; the King was not sorry at all and got around to hiring Inigo Jones to design a masterpiece.

The building of the new Banqueting House finished in 1622 and ended up being a nod to what the King referred to whilst praising Lord Sinclair's banquet. Banqueting House is a marvel that still stands today open in London to visitors from across the world. The ceiling has breathtaking Rubens paintings that pay homage to the divine right of Kings, amongst other things. Built in the Italian Renaissance style, it astonished all those who surveyed it and still does today. Rubens managed to get paid for his work, albeit late, also receiving a gold chain for his services.

The magnificent hall was also home to 'The King's Evil'. A belief that the King had the power to heal, or at least prevent, a nasty skin disorder that became known as the King's Evil. Sufferers could be cured by the touch of the monarch. This annual ritual used to take place in the opulent surroundings of the Banqueting House.

CHAPTER EIGHTEEN

The Earl of Bothwell

The troubled visitor in the night desperate to see Lord Sinclair was already on the run for plotting against the King, but what followed the banquet was a turn for the worse. He lived on the run for two years but was eventually captured in 1591 and was arrested with fresh charges of witchcraft after being named by some witches in the North Berwick Witch trials. He was imprisoned in Edinburgh Castle, close to the King and his armed forces.

As he always seemed to have a knack of doing, he escaped a few months later whilst the King and most of his armed forces were away for a wedding. He was seething as he was convinced that Lord Maitland was behind the accusation. Within 3 days, he was named an outlaw. The King's forces searched high and low for him including interrogating his household staff but the Earl was bold and stayed hidden until he broke into Holyroodhouse attempting to reconcile with the King, according to him, whilst others felt he wanted to assassinate the King. The

Earl was driven away in a bloody battle.

1592 came and there were reports that the Earl was hiding at his mother's house. The King and his armed forces raced to the house, but during the journey, the King's horse threw him into a pool of water so the chase had to be abandoned.

The Earl didn't enjoy being an outlaw and wrote a letter to the Clergy fiercely denying the charges of witchcraft. In April 1592, there were reports of the Earl holed up near Dundee, so the King and his armed forces raced to the scene only to end up empty handed again. The Earl had been tipped off by traitors from within the King's inner circle.

In June 1592, the Scottish Parliament sat for the first time in five years and the first item of business was to strip the Earl of his titles and land. The Earl didn't take too kindly to this, so along with 300 of his men stormed the King's castle to capture the King. This time the King was the one who was tipped off so his castle and men were waiting and able to defend the fortress.

The King's strategy changed and all of the Earl's supporters and known accomplices were arrested and imprisoned. This continued throughout 1592 and by the early part of 1593, the Earl was in the North of England and was seen as the anti-King James which was propping up his support and enabled him to evade capture for so long.

In the Summer of 1593, The Earl smuggled himself into the King's bedroom within Holyroodhouse, much like he had done on the night of the banquet - although this time it was deliberate! The Earl didn't want to harm the King, but wanted to protest his innocence and promise his loyalty to the King. The King accepted this - it was better to have the Earl on his side than a rival. He was formally acquitted in a trial shortly afterwards.

The King however took council from those against the Earl and changed his mind. Whilst the Earl would be pardoned, he was to be exiled and would have to leave Scotland. The Earl didn't comply and again built a rebellion against the King.

This continued into 1594 with bloody battles between the King's and the Earl's armed forces. In May, Anne of Denmark's jewels were stolen, and the Earl found the culprit and recovered some jewels, hoping to use this as a bargaining chip. The King's men refused the Earl's offer to bring the culprit back to Scotland. The English Ambassador also refused to help the Earl.

This lack of support continued, and the Earl was seen as weak and yesterday's man. In the autumn of 1594, further charges were brought against him for being a Protestant.

The Earl continued to hide and lurk in the shadows into 1595, but was living in poverty. He was rumoured to have been hiding out on the island of Orkney, part of Scotland.

He then made his way to France, but when the King heard about this, he asked France to banish him, but they refused. Bothwell didn't feel welcomed and moved on after several months to Spain.

He was rumoured to have visited London during 1598, but the King didn't believe it.

Eventually, the Earl moved to Naples in Italy, where he passed away in 1612. He died shortly after the Prince of Wales, King James's heir to the throne. This crushed the Earl's spirits because he believed that the Prince would have restored his titles and land had he ascended to the throne. While he died penniless, he had a grand funeral paid for by the Spanish who ruled Naples.

CHAPTER NINETEEN

Lord Sinclair and Knockhall Castle

L ord Sinclair was not a young man when the banquet took place, being aged 62 years old, but he was far from finished. He ended up being a judge in the trial of the Earl of Bothwell when he was formally acquitted and continued to have an influence despite his advancing years. It is documented that he attended a reception for the Dutch Ambassador in 1594.

The King didn't like to have the Scottish Parliament open too often, as he didn't welcome too much of a democratic debate. Instead, he held *Conventions of Estate*, which was like Parliament but would be called by the King only for raising taxes. Lord Sinclair was present at the Conventions of Dunfermline in 1596, Holyrood 1597, and Dundee 1597.

He did eventually pass away in 1601, aged c.85 years old. An incredible feat for a man born in the 16th Century.

Lady Sinclair outlived him passing away in 1607, aged

61.

In terms of the impressive Knockhall Castle, it stayed in the Sinclair family until 1634 when it was purchased by the Udny family. They were the barons of the Udny region in Aberdeenshire, and this Castle was perfectly located for them. The Castle didn't seem to fare well under the Udny reign. After only five years, the Castle was severely damaged when it was loaned out to the Covenanters, an offshoot of the Protestants.

The Covenanters were so called because of the bond between God and the Israelites in the Old Testament. They started in the mid 1550s and grew in strength, which culminated in a period of turmoil shortly after the Udny family loaned the Castle to them. King Charles and the Archbishop of Canterbury were pressuring the Scots to accept a different way of practising religion that was not something that the Covenanters were prepared to do. This led to bloody armed battles for several years, with Knockhall Castle being one casualty. By the late 17th Century, they had more or less been crushed with their beliefs subsumed into other religious offshoots.

As for Knockhall Castle, it was returned to the Udny family after the Covenanters had been driven out of Aberdeenshire and the family worked hard to restore the castle. They lived there happily until 1734 when a fire gutted the entire Castle, just leaving the bare structure in place. The Castle has remained a ruin ever since and can still be visited. In 2019, the Castle was put on sale for £130,000 or around $150,000. Not much to own such a historic castle. However, it is a protected site meaning that any work to it would need to maintain its ruins so the cost of restoring the Castle to its former glories would be a considerable amount. Along with the slow process of gaining planning permission each step of the way. It remains empty to this day.

CHAPTER TWENTY

The Maitlands

L ord Maitland was a powerful man at the time of the banquet with a beautiful wife that was the envy of many. A few months after the banquet, Lord Maitland joined King James on his journey to collect Anne of Denmark. He did more than just accompany the King, as he was also responsible for the financing and accounting for the journey. Anne's mother also asked him to help set up Anne's household in Scotland.

Lord Maitland picked up more titles from the King in recognition of his service, becoming a Lord of Parliament with the title Lord Maitland of Thirlestane in 1590.

It is also documented that Lord Maitland came to the rescue of the King in 1591 during a household strike when all the kitchen staff left their posts, much like they did during the banquet. Lord Maitland used all of his negotiating skills to bring them back to work.

All of this power, influence, and recognition meant that Anne resented him. She also blamed him in 1593 for starting rumours that she had an affair and was supporting the Earl of Bothwell. Anne was furious and demanded that King James take the lands of Musselburgh and Inveresk away from Lord Maitland, as she believed she was entitled to it. He did as he was asked and transferred these to her.

The situation had become so toxic that in 1594, King James appealed to Anne's brother for her to give Maitland another chance articulating that Lord Maitland was helpful and loyal. Sadly, the tension continued, and he passed away in 1595, aged 58. King James wrote the epitaph. He was a loss to the entire country.

As for Lady Maitland, upon her husband's death she quickly became a rich widow. It didn't take her long to remarry the Earl of Cassilis who was some 22 years younger than her, which caused quite a stir.

Anne forgave her for the rumours, and they were wonderful friends by 1595. Her wealth meant that she kept influence in the Scottish court despite the scandal of her marriage.

In 1600, Lady Maitland (or the Countess of Cassilis as she was now known) along with her husband hosted the King for a banquet at Thirlestane Castle, one can only wonder whether it was as eventful or impactful on history as the banquet that Lord Sinclair hosted for the King.

She was referred to as a 'lady without all religion' in 1602 for her lifestyle. More scandal was to erupt in 1604 when her husband was twice imprisoned for violence against her. The first time was when he dragged her from court in front of countless witnesses. King James was always loyal to those who were loyal to him and even though it was nearly 10 years after Lord Maitland's death, he ensured that her finances were protected from any power grab by the Earl.

She passed away in 1609 after a brief illness aged 63, being buried near her first husband, Lord Maitland.

CHAPTER TWENTY-ONE

Anne of Denmark

After the formal marriage in November 1589, a month of celebrations followed before the happy couple spent a prolonged honeymoon firstly visiting Anne's family at Kronborg Castle, where a young Anne spent a happy childhood. The couple then spent some time in Copenhagen attending the wedding of Anne's older sister. This took them through into May 1590 when Anne made her formal debut in Edinburgh in a silver coach bought over from Denmark with King James riding alongside on horseback.

Her coronation was a major event with her becoming the first Protestant Queen in Scotland. It was Lord Maitland who placed the crown upon her head.

Anne and King James were madly in love, but after his eye wandered, she changed her demeanour and her happiness dissipated. Anne was also heartbroken that their firstborn, Prince Henry, was kept away from her to prepare him for his first steps to becoming King. In 1594, she began a campaign to regain custody of Prince Harry garnering the support of Lord Maitland, who perhaps wanted to get her on side. King James refused and instructed his staff to never allow Prince Henry to be alone in Anne's company. This reached a climax in 1595 when Anne suffered a miscarriage and then withdrew into her shell, giving up her campaign for custody. Anne did eventually gain custody when King James moved to London, as this was her demand to join him in England.

There were rumours that Anne had enough of King James and plotted with conspirators against the King. In 1600, she was linked to a plot to assassinate the King. Her ladies-in-waiting were dismissed for their link to the plot, but Anne refused to support the dismissal. She remained in bed for two days, refusing to eat until they were reinstated. King James even hired a famous acrobat to entertain her. Eventually he folded and agreed to reinstate the ladies-in-waiting, which alarmed the Government who viewed that as a security risk.

Anne didn't like King James's drinking and frequently commented on it. The couple lived apart after 1607, with Anne moving between residences. The death of Prince Henry in 1612 hit Anne very hard, and she never recovered from it. Her health deteriorated, and she was rarely seen in public.

There was however a bizarre confrontation in 1613 when Anne shot the King's favourite dog during a hunting session, which caused a massive argument. Eventually, the King, not Anne apologised, with him giving Anne a £2,000 diamond in memory of his dog who was called Jewel.

In 1614, she had pain in her feet which worsened into 1615 and she was thought to have dropsy, an illness where excess fluid is stored within the body. She continued on with her conditioning worsening in 1617, finding it difficult to move.

Anne did however go on a shopping trip to Central London which drew quite a crowd and also was prescribed an odd treatment by her Doctor. She was told to saw wood as it would improve the blood flow but sadly it just made her more tired. Eventually, she passed away in 1619.

Although King James visited Anne only three times during his illness, he was distraught by her death. He was heartbroken and was seen sighing, fainting, and was truly broken. She was buried in Westminster Abbey in London.

During her life, she gave birth to seven children who survived childbirth, but four of them died in childhood.

CHAPTER TWENTY-TWO

The Others

The Ambassador

The Ambassador was already in declining health, so he sadly passed away a year after the banquet. He didn't leave much financially in his estate. He never used his political connections to benefit himself financially or to create business ties for his own purposes. Instead, he viewed his role as one of State, and an honour that would have been cheapened had he used it as a tool to enrich himself.

Andrew Melville.

Andrew was devastated by the death of his wife and found it difficult to gain closure given the exposure that the North Berwick witch trials had for several years. After Jane's death, he remained loyal to the King and was a key part in protecting the King, including the episode when the Earl of Bothwell attacked Holyroodhouse in 1591.

He continued to work for King James and was knighted in 1604 and then retired to his own country mansion. In 1611, his pension was further topped up by

King James, ever grateful and loyal to those who were loyal to him. Andrew eventually passed away in 1617 when he was in his mid-70s.

William Fowler.

William continued to be close to the King, he became Private Secretary and Master of Requests for Anne post the marriage and continued to write poetry. His account of the baptism of Prince Henry and the banquet & celebrations that took place in 1594 were similar to what happened in the banquet that took place at Knockhall Castle.

In 1598, William became a spy for the English Court, sending back secret messages to Queen Elizabeth. It is unclear whether King James ever found out about this or whether it was uncovered in the history books many years later.

William fell in love in 1603 with Arabella Stuart and wrote two poems for her including *Upon an Horologe of the Clock at Loseley* which includes a partial anagram of her name and described her as the eight wonder of the world.

As mentioned earlier, in 1611 King James granted William 2,000 acres (8 Sq Km) of land in Ulster as a reward for his service. Most of the land he received was in an area called Moyglass, and the islands of Inishfomer, Galleran, and Lougherne. He sold it all in 1615 to Sir John Hume.

He passed away in 1613, aged 52. He was always fond of jewellery, as per his poem to the King at the banquet, so the jewels he received from Anne and King James over his years of service were bequeathed to his Brother.

His collection of poems remains in the library of the University of Edinburgh.

Mark Alexander Boyd

The King's artistic influence really inspired Mark who wrote his best work in 1590 and 1592 whilst living in South West France. He returned to Scotland in 1596 and passed away in 1601, aged only 39. He is now best remembered for one poem, the *Sonnet of Venus and Cupid.*

The Moore

The Moore stole the show at the banquet and is thought to have also performed at the entry of Queen Anne in 1590. William Fowler's account of the baptism of Prince Henry in 1594 also listed The Moore as performing a similar routine to that as seen at the banquet at Knockhall Castle. He is listed as *The Moir* in Anne's records as being a member of her household but sadly there are no further records so it remains a mystery what happened to him.

See Photos And Portraits Of Some Of The People, Places And Events That Occurred In The Book Including:

- Knockhall Castle
- King James VI
- Anne of Denmark
- Lord Maitland
- The North Berwick Witch Trials
- The New World Expedition
- King James VI's lovers

Just go to http://www.derekgorman.com. You can also get added to my mailing list to find out when my next book will be released and get in touch with me

Message From The Author:

Hopefully, you found this book entertaining whilst also learning about the impact that King James made on the world, and gaining a glimpse into the real lives of the supporting cast.

The best way to say thank-you to me if you enjoyed this book would be to **please leave a review on Amazon**, this would justify all those countless hours over an entire year to get this book done and will motivate me to write another one.

[1] A Counterblaste to Tobacco, King James VI and I, 1604.

BIBLIOGRAPHY

As is typical in the modern world, the Internet played the key role in research and whilst this novel strived to be accurate and influenced by history, as described in the prologue, it isn't a non-fiction, historical book. It will therefore be no surprise that Wikipedia was the principal source, including the following pages on Wikipedia - there may be some others I haven't listed

- King James
- Anne of Denmark
- Lord Sinclair
- Lord Maitland
- Jean Fleming
- William Fowler
- Mark Alexander Boyd
- Jane Kennedy
- Thomas Randolph - the Ambassador
- Knockhall Castle
- Clan Udny
- Coronation of Anne
- Masque at baptism of Henry
- James VI personal relationships
- North Berwick Witch Trials

- Banquo and Macbeth
- Divine right of kings
- Plantation of Ulster
- Castalian Band

Other significant sources included these websites:

- Cassidycash.com - instructions on playing noddy | True Law of Free Monarchies - https://www.bl.uk/collection-items/the-true-law-of-free-monarchies-by-king-james-vi-and-i
- Daemonologie | https://www.bl.uk/collection-items/king-james-vi-and-is-demonology-1597
- Scotland landscape in the 16th Century | https://www.thereformation.info/scotland16c/
- Tudor Dining in the 16th Century | https://www.historyextra.com/period/tudor/tudor-dining-a-guide-to-food-and-status-in-the-16th-century/
- Tower of London Menagerie | https://www.hrp.org.uk/tower-of-london/history-and-stories/the-tower-of-london-menagerie/#gs.ym0tia
- King James Finances | https://www.historylearningsite.co.uk/stuart-england/james-i-and-royal-revenue/
- Banqueting House | https://www.hrp.org.uk/banqueting-house/history-and-stories/the-story-of-banqueting-house/#gs.0lx2oy
- Life in a Castle | https://www.english-heritage.org.uk/castles/life-in-a-castle/
- Andrew Melville of Garvick | http://venitap.com/Genealogy/WebCards/ps48/ps48_433.html
- Lord Sinclair | http://www.cracroftspeerage.co.uk/

online/content/sinclair1677.htm
- History of King James and Tobacco | https://medium.com/historys-ink/an-introduction-to-this-vile-habit-king-james-counter-blast-to-tobacco-9c985373b2ac
- Holinshed Chronicle | https://www.canterbury-cathedral.org/heritage/archives/picture-this/holinsheds-chronicles-macbeth-banquo-and-three-weird-sisters-ccl-w-g-5-15/
- Knockhall Castle - Estate Agent | https://search.savills.com/property-detail/gbabrsabs160078
- Knockhall Castle | https://canmore.org.uk/site/20348/knockhall-castle

Printed in Great Britain
by Amazon